CREATION SCIENCE CLUB

Challenging Ms. Eva Lution

John and Lisa Fox

Challenging Ms. Eva Lution
The Creation Science Club: Book 1
by John and Lisa Fox

First printing: January 2016

ISBN 978-1-942773-00-9
Cover design: Abel Hernandez
Design and layout: Keaton Halley
Style and proofreading: Dr. Robert Carter and Lita Cosner

Published by:

CREATION BOOK PUBLISHERS

Creation Book Publishers
P.O. Box 350
Powder Springs, GA, 30127, USA.
Phone: 1-800-616-1264
creationbookpublishers.com

We dedicate this book
to all the members of our family
who are colored by the rainbow
of the Autism Spectrum.

We also want to thank:

Buddy Davis, whose creation music ministry and dinosaur sculpting first inspired us to dig deeper into the truth,

Jonathan Sarfati, who has written books to refute the endless barrage of evolution's 'overwhelming evidence' coming at us from every side,

Creation Ministries International, for providing us all with various resources and an endless supply of 'scientific stones of truth' for our slings.

With special gratitude to Dr. Robert Carter, Lita Cosner, and others at CMI for taking the time to review this book.

*Note: If any errors or misuse of terms or facts
occur in this series, these mistakes are solely
the responsibility of the authors.

PART 1

The Origin of the Universe

CHAPTER 1

*Faster…faster…*his lungs were burning, and his legs were numb, but David knew he wasn't running fast enough. He could hear the crashing branches and the steady huffing of its breath not far behind him. David knew that somewhere up ahead was a cabin. It was his only hope. If he could just make it there…*if he could just make it…*

Pushing through the woodsy undergrowth, David made a sudden turn and ducked under a low branch…*Wham!* Something fell right behind him, then…*Bam!* He ran full force into a wall of immovable bars that had appeared in front of him. He was knocked to the ground before he knew what was happening.

The chase was over. Spinning around on his back pockets, David faced the giant beast rising up before him. Nearly six feet tall, it had to weigh close to 300 pounds. Step by step, the bear closed the gap between them. Ten feet…eight feet…six feet…then, it stopped. The angry bear huffed and growled, but couldn't get any closer. Thick bamboo bars separated it from the exhausted boy.

****

David had given up calling for help nearly an hour ago and he'd given up trying brute force an hour before that. Intelligence and ingenuity had not yet gotten him free, so he figured just waiting was his best bet.

Looking through the bamboo bars, David sighed. Actually, he wasn't really upset. He was definitely happier being trapped inside a bamboo cage than being trapped inside a big black bear. As crazy as it sounds, he was almost as glad just to be missing the last few hours of school.

David sat down and let out a deeper sigh. The events of the last few hours reminded him a little too much of the last few weeks of his life. He had been running—afraid of losing yet another fight. He was just about ready to give up and find a cage he could lock himself away in to hide. He was just too worn out and frustrated.

His parents had warned him that middle school would be more challenging than elementary school. He thought he was ready. He honestly thought he was prepared. But now, he realized that *nothing* could have prepared him for his eighth grade honors science class.

Leaning his head back against the bars, David prayed, "Lord, I want to believe the Bible. But science class seems to be confusing the faith right out of me. If You're really there, I need You to send me some kind of help. I just don't think I can fight this anymore."

David hadn't closed his eyes while praying, so, even before saying, "amen," he caught sight of a bit of color heading his way through the underbrush. It wasn't long before two older boys were standing there looking through the bars at him.

Both boys looked pretty disappointed. "You aren't a bear," the one on the right said.

David had to laugh. "Nope. You got me there. I'm not a bear."

Both boys cocked their heads to the left at the same time and smiled. David felt like he was seeing double. The boys looked exactly alike—identical twins.

Twin on the right then turned to twin on the left and said, "I guess you owe me 20 bucks. My trap worked."

Twin on the left replied, "Wrong, wrong, wrong. If anything, *you* owe *me* 20 bucks. I bet you that your trap couldn't catch a *bear*. And, as you can see, it didn't catch a bear—it caught a kid."

David squinted a bit at the twins. He felt a little concern rising inside of him. These guys weren't quite your average teens. There was definitely something different about them. "Um, excuse me. Could you guys let me out? My parents are gonna be worried about me if I don't get home soon."

Twin on the left seemed to think this was an okay idea. So, he walked over to one side of the cage and pulled a thin piece of wood out of his back pocket. When he inserted the wood into a slot, it released the mechanism that had kept the door securely locked. "Look," he said, "I'll just hang the *key* right here on this branch. That way, if you ever get stuck in here again, you can let yourself out."

"Thanks, man," David said as he stepped out of the cage, "but I don't plan on running into *this* trap again. Besides, I didn't think it was legal to trap bears around here."

Twin on the right snickered. "Code 422 of the current Greenville trapping laws states, 'if a bear is causing damage to property, live trapping is not only acceptable, but encouraged. However, anything trapped must be immediately, within two hours of discovery, reported to the Greenville Animal Control for removal and relocation.'" With that, he pulled out his cell phone and started *beeping* away.

David turned to Left Twin. "Who's he calling?"

"Well, the Greenville Animal Control, of course. We have to immediately report your capture for removal and relocation."

David raised his hands. "Whoa! I don't think…"

Left Twin busted out laughing as Right Twin snapped his phone shut. "Did you see his face, Darin?" Left Twin said. "Man, you got him good!"

Right Twin was laughing so hard he started to snort. Then he reached out his hand toward David. "My name's Darin Tadue. And this is my brother, Abel."

"Well, hey," David shook each boy's hand. "My name's David Avila. And your trap, here, actually saved my life. No joke! This big ol' bear almost had me! Then, I ran into this thing, the door slammed shut, and the bear decided to give up and go away." He looked around a bit nervously. "I didn't think bears ever came this close to town."

Abel and Darin got serious real quick. "Whoa, dude! It's a good thing that bear didn't catch you. If it's gonna start chasing people, we might have to give up on trying to trap it and just have Billy shoot it."

"Who's Billy?" David asked, looking around again.

Abel pointed down the hill. "Billy owns the cabin down there."

Then Darin pointed up the hill. "He also owns the old meat shed up yonder. We use it to store some of the chemicals and things for our experiments."

"It also has a couple of freezers in it to store some of the food and things for our eating," Abel added.

"But that bear keeps breaking in and causing trouble." Darin shook his head. "It ate ten frozen pizzas last week—we had just stocked up."

"Not to mention he trashed the freezer," Abel scowled. "It took us two days to get it working again."

"So, anyway," David asked, "what school you guys go to?"

Darin waved his hands in front of himself as if he were chasing away flies. "School-schmool," he said rolling his eyes. "We've been done with school since we were 12."

"No way!" David said. "I sure wish I were done with school!"

"Actually, we're really still in school." Abel explained, "Right now we're working on our Master's Degrees in the biological sciences."

"Master's Degrees! Like how old are you guys, anyway?"

"We're both 17," Darin answered. "I was 15 when I received my B.S. in Biology." Then he added with a smirk, "But poor Abel, here, was 16 and 38 days before he got his."

Abel responded by swatting Darin on the arm. "That's only because I was in the hospital for two weeks after you talked me into testing out your free-floating flyer!"

Darin swatted Abel back—twice. "Well, it's your fault it didn't work!"

Then Abel made a dive for Darin. "My fault? I'll show you whose fault it was!"

David just stood there watching the brothers tussle on the ground. Neither seemed angry. Both just seemed to be enjoying the moment. David wasn't quite sure what to do…

"Okay, knock it off, you two," a loud, but friendly voice called out. A big man with a big smile pushed his way through the bushes into the small clearing. The man looked at David and then at the mess he had made trying to dig his way out of the cage. "Looks like you guys caught one mighty small bear. I really don't think he's the one that's been raiding the meat shed."

Everyone laughed, and the man held out his hand to David. "My name's Billy James. These two been givin' you trouble?"

David shook Billy's hand. "I'm David Avila. And, no, sir, no trouble. Actually, I'm glad I got trapped in there. It ended up saving me from two big bears."

"Two?" the twins gasped.

Billy's big smile faded. "I didn't know we had *two* bears up here."

David shook his head and smiled. "No. I guess that's not what I meant. There really was a big bear up here. And it chased me right into Darin and Abel's trap. Man, was I ever scared—*way scared!* But the other *bear* I was talking about is my science teacher. I'd almost rather face that real bear again than go to my science class."

Abel and Darin both looked shocked. "You don't like science class? How can anyone not like science? I mean, we could give you ten-million-kazillion reasons to like science."

Billy held up a hand. "Whoa, guys! How about instead we just ask David why *he* doesn't like science."

David shrugged his shoulders. "It's not that I don't *like* science. Actually, I love science. It's just that my science teacher and I really don't see eye to eye on some issues."

"Like…?" Darin asked.

David hesitated, but then explained. "Well, uh, you see, my teacher is *all* evolution. She says the Bible and talk about a Creator don't have anything to do with science. And, well, my dad's a pastor…and so, my family believes what the Bible says…that God's the Creator of everything."

Abel and Darin crossed their arms and tightened their lips. "Uh, oh," David thought, "here it comes…again."

"Good for you!" the brothers said in unison.

David was shocked. "What? You mean it?" He turned to Billy to make sure the twins weren't just teasing him.

Billy gave David another big grin. "I can see you're not used to getting that response. But they really do mean it. As a matter a fact, the guys and I have been toying with the idea of starting a Creation Science Club—you know, finding scientific evidence that points to biblical creation rather than secular evolution."

"That's so totally cool!" David said. "Where do I sign up to join?"

Billy laughed as Abel and Darin came over to slap David on the back—a bit over-enthusiastically. "So," Billy asked, "you been in that cage all day?"

"Nah. You see, if I cut over Maple Hill and through the field, I can just make it home and back for lunch—if I run. So, I was on my way back from lunch, and I guess that bear must have decided to have *me* for *its* lunch."

"More likely," Billy guessed, "the bear smelled what you'd had for lunch and wanted to get some for himself.

"Anyway, just a bit down the hill is our cabin. You can grab a drink, then you should probably call your parents. The school might have contacted them about you by now. Then, if it's okay with your folks, we'll give you a ride home so you won't have to worry about facing any more bears."

"Sounds great," David said. "Thanks."

On the way down the hill, Darin talked nonstop to David about the bear-sensor he was designing and how he planned to add a night-vision monitor. All the while, Abel, at the very same time, talked to David about his growing repertoire of famous voices he could mimic—giving examples of each. David felt pretty overwhelmed. But Billy James just smiled and whistled a quiet tune to himself. It was obvious he was used to this.

CHAPTER 2

The following week, Billy pulled his jeep up to the Maple Hill cabin. But before he even reached the cabin door, an excited voice called through the window. "Hey, Billy! Hurry up! Come check out the *Invention of the Century*. It's fan-awesome-tastic!"

Striding into the cabin, Billy grinned. "So, Darin, you and Abel have finally finished your secret invention. Let's see how *fan-awesome-tastic* it really is."

Seemingly out of nowhere, the voice of Engineer Montgomery Scott spoke out. "Admiral, prepare yourself to be impressed. In all my years on the Enterprise, I have yet to see such technology." Billy and Darin weren't surprised by the voice. They were used to Abel imitating all sorts of voices.

Billy looked eagerly at the invention in Darin's hand. After a moment of silence, he commented, "Uh, it just looks like a clipboard to me."

Darin and Abel slapped each other on the back and chuckled. "Right, right!" Darin said excitedly. "That's what makes it so cool. It *looks* like an ordinary clipboard, but it's *really*—a *Computer Tutor!* You see, we heard that the public schools really need science tutors. So, Abel and I invented these. I plan to sell them to all the schools. Soon, we'll be rolling in the bucks!"

"Well, Darin, I seem to remember hearing *that* before," Billy said, shaking his head. "But you're right, the schools do need science tutors. You know, as hard as the teachers try, there's nothing like one-on-one attention to catch a student's interest."

"And, believe me! Nothing will catch their interest like our Computer Tutor," Darin boasted. "Okay, Scotty, turn on the power and let's show the Admiral what she can do!"

Billy, Abel, and Darin all leaned forward to see the clipboard computer prove its worth.

Engineer Scott was the first to speak. "Well, Cap'n, could you explain to us the meaning of that upside-down question mark?"

"What! Give me that!" Darin said, grabbing the clipboard computer back. "Oh no! This is the worst thing that could have happened! It means we've lost everything. Blunder-thunder and unceasing sorrow! It's gonna take forever to reload it all!"

"Don't worry, Darin," Billy said, patting his despairing friend on the back. "I think you were right to want to help the kids. So, while you're fixing your computer-tutor gizmo, why don't we go ahead and volunteer as real living science tutors down at Darwin Middle School?"

Darin looked worried. "*Darwin* Middle School?" he asked. "As in Charles Darwin, the *father of evolution*?"

Billy smiled mischievously. "That's right. Sounds like an exciting challenge, doesn't it?" Then he went whistling out of the room.

Abel whispered to Darin, "Cap'n, sounds like we'll be entering enemy territory."

****

The next Monday, Billy, Darin, and Abel filed into Darwin Middle School's science room. They quietly found three open seats among the other students and tutors. As soon as they were seated, a stern-faced, thirty-something woman entered the room. "Hello, everyone," the woman said without smiling. "I am Ms. Eva Lution, the principal and eighth grade honors science teacher here at Darwin Middle School."

"Oh, no!" Darin whispered in a panicky voice. "Did you hear her name? This is getting scarier every minute—first *Darwin School*, now, *Eva Lution*."

Ms. Lution continued without noticing Darin. "I am very pleased to see so many tutors willing to help our honors students with their series of science reports." Her eyes scanned the room as she spoke. "The school board has recently raised the bar on scholastic excellence. By the end of this class, students will be able to clearly answer today's most important science questions."

Abel raised his hand enthusiastically. Ms. Lution seemed irritated at being interrupted, but responded, "Yes, young man, do you have a question?"

"Yes, m'am. I was wondering what you meant by *today's most important science questions*?"

Ms. Lution rubbed her hand on the back of her neck, trying to decide if she should answer this boy's question or just ask him to keep quiet. "Well, of course, I can't take the time to spell it all out right now. But here are a few examples of what I mean: How and when did the universe come into being? Wh..."

"Oh, oh, oh!" Darin was now waving his hand eagerly in the air. "I know, I know the answer."

Ms. Lution was too surprised to say anything. She just looked at him, so he continued, "How and when did the universe come into being? The answer's in Genesis. It tells us what God did and when: 'In the beginning, God created the heavens and the earth.'"

Ms. Lution sighed. "Young man, this is science class, *not* Sunday School. *Real* scientists know that the universe began with the big bang billions of years ago. And, from there, the earth took approximately 4.6 billion years of evolution to form all that we see today."

Darin didn't seem at all offended by Ms. Lution's curt words. He just smiled and politely responded, "Excuse me, but how do you *know* that the earth took billions of years to form?" Then he shrugged his shoulders and added, "I mean, were you *there* to see it happen?"

Ms. Eva Lution's face turned red as she glanced around the room at all the students and tutors waiting to hear her answer. "No, I wasn't!" she answered, trying to control her temper. "But neither were you. No one was. The human race didn't even begin to evolve until 1.6 million years ago." She rolled her eyes. "*Real* scientists look at the facts for answers—not children's stories."

"Well," Billy James spoke up, "I am a *real* scientist. And as a real scientist, I *do* look closely at the facts. Yet, as a Christian, I also choose to believe the eyewitness account of the One who was there—God the Creator. I start with what He says in the Bible and go from there to..."

"*Sir*," Ms. Lution interrupted Billy in a no-nonsense tone, "you have a right to your own religious beliefs. But that's all they are, just *beliefs*. On the other hand, the big bang and evolution are facts, supported by overwhelming, solid, scientific evidence."

"Excuse me, Ms. Lution, m'am," a boy from the back spoke up. It was David Avila, the boy from the bear trap.

"My dad says that the Bible is true. He says that the big bang and evolution are just beliefs—and that nothing has ever been found to prove that they're true. He says that if scientists would look objectively at the facts, they'd see that the evidence confirms biblical creation a lot more than it does the theory of evolution." David looked over at Billy and smiled.

Abel and Darin practically jumped out of their seats, they were so excited to see David. However, Ms. Lution's tone put a damper on the reunion. "Yes, David," she replied impatiently, "we all know that your father is a pastor and that he teaches you those things. However, as your science teacher, it is my job to show you the *scientific* facts of evolution, not to just let you believe whatever you're told."

Billy turned toward David, and said, "You know, David, she's right. While it's good and right to believe our parents, there comes a time when we ourselves have to look closely at the evidence and find out *why* we believe something is true."

"But," David asked, "isn't it right that I should just believe the Bible by faith?"

Billy spoke kindly, but confidently. "Yes, David, sometimes we have to hold onto the truth by faith alone. However, in many cases, God gives us the means to show that what we believe is...believable. The Bible itself says that we should be ready to explain why we think what we believe is true. That's why..."

"Yes, yes, yes," Ms. Lution interrupted, waving her hand back and forth. "That's why we're writing these honors science reports—to show *all* of you the overwhelming, scientific evidence that evolution is true. I assure you that thousands of topnotch scientists from the finest universities have put in a hundred lifetimes of research confirming what we will be learning this year in this honors class."

Then, walking back up to the front of the room, she continued in her no-nonsense tone. "Now, students, quickly take a moment to pair up with a tutor. We've wasted a lot of time with all this nonsense."

David gathered his things and went over to take the seat between Billy and Darin. Darin patted him on the back and whispered, "You sure were brave to tell Ms. Lution that you believe the Bible."

Abel added, "Maybe your parents should have named you *Daniel,* for, like, facing the lion's den."

David blushed and laughed. "Actually, my dad named me David to encourage me to fight against the *giants* that are in the world today. I think evolution is one of those *giants*."

"You're more right than you know," Billy explained. "Evolution, with its big bang and millions and billions of years, is a lot like the giant Goliath. It's grown to be so big and strong that it even scares some Christians. They don't know how to fight it, so they just hide whenever their faith in God's Word is challenged."

David sighed. "I sure know how that feels."

"Well," Billy smiled, "now we can face and fight this giant together."

****

Once the meeting was over, Billy, Abel, and Darin waited outside with David for his mom to come and pick him up. Darin opened up a metal box in the back of Billy's jeep and pulled out a pair of large, visor-like sunglasses. "These are my *R.M.* glasses—that stands for *Reality Morphing*," he explained with one eyebrow raised. "They kinda like turn life into an interactive video game. Abel and I have programmed them with all sorts of themes." Then, after pressing a few buttons on the side of the glasses, he put them on David and said, "Now, David-dude, check out Abel."

David turned to look at Abel, but instead he found himself staring up at a nine-foot tall giant, complete with a spear, shield, and sword. "Awesome!"

The giant bent down toward David, waving his sword in his face. "Who do you think you are? You're nothing but a pup yipping at my heels!" Goliath (Abel) let out a loud, mocking laugh, "Ha, ha ha! Nobody's gonna listen to you. Everyone believes in evolution…not your Creator…ha ha ha!"

David took off the glasses with a disturbed look on his face. "It really does seem like everyone believes in evolution. I mean, every book I've ever read and every nature program I've ever seen talks about evolution like it's a fact."

Darin's face fell, and he said with a sigh, "Yep, it's the crafty work of media-mania."

"Media-mania?" David asked. "What do you mean?"

"I think what Darin's trying to say," Billy answered, "is that the media supports evolution and puts it everywhere for everyone to see. News programs, library books, encyclopedias, textbooks, TV shows, even movies—they all present evolution as scientific fact. They make it *seem* that everyone believes in the 'science' of evolution, and that belief in the Bible is outdated and 'unscientific.'"

"But," Darin jumped in, "that's just not the reality." He continued excitedly, "A recent poll showed that the majority of people in America actually reject evolution, even though public education and media-mania have been cramming it down our throats for decades."

"The majority *doesn't* believe in evolution?" David questioned.

Abel nodded emphatically. "And—get this—it's not just the 'regular' people rejecting evolution. The fact is, hundreds and hundreds of highly-educated scientists have also rejected the theory of evolution as… impossible, preposterous, ridiculous—even crazy!"

"Really?" David turned to Billy.

"Yep!" Billy smiled. "And, it's not just the Christian or religious scientists that are rejecting evolution. You see, when scientists take an honest, earnest look at the evidence for and against evolution, they realize that it just can't be the answer.

"Anyway," Billy summarized, "it doesn't really matter what the majority says. The whole world could reject the Creator, but we have the truth in the Word of God."

****

The next day, David met with his new friends at Favorite Flavors ice cream shop to make plans on how to research and write his first science report.

Having already finished their sundaes, Darin and Abel watched David as he finished his own five-dip-triple-topping-whipped-cream-with-two-cherries-banana-split. They cheered him on, "You can do it, dude! Don't give up!"

With a triumphant smile, David downed his last bite, and the twins burst into loud applause. Billy reached out to shake his hand, saying, "Well, you did it. You passed the test. That makes you an official member of the Creation Science Club, or CSC for short. I guess that makes this our first official CSC meeting. So, we'd better get down to some serious business. David, do you have the guidelines for your first science report?"

"Yep, right here in my backpack."

Glancing through the guidelines, Billy said, "So, looks like the topic for your first report is *The Origin of the Universe*. I guess Ms. Lution wants a foundational report on which the rest of your 'evolution' reports can be based."

Darin snickered, "Hey, David-dude, are you gonna have a surprise for her or what?"

Abel was a little more serious as he morphed his voice into a Scottish accent, "Well, David-lad, are you thinkin' you'll be ready to go where no Darwin student has gone before?"

David smiled, but was equally serious with his answer. "My dad told me I'd better be prepared for some *enemy fire*."

"Anyway," Billy pulled them back to the guidelines, "for research, it says here we have to visit at least two information sources from Ms. Lution's list, and then we have to pick a third of our own. With the information we gather, you need to have a five-page report ready by the end of two weeks." Looking up at the others, Billy asked, "Well, which of these sources looks good to you guys?"

"Hey, would you look at that," Abel said pointing to the list. "That's our friend Dr. Veritas's museum. See? *The Museum of Certain Science*."

"Wow, he's got a cool name!" David exclaimed. "I'll bet you guys already know that *veritas* means *truth* in Latin."

"Yeah, yeah," Darin wagged his head back and forth. "It's too bad that Dr. Veritas doesn't live up to his name."

Billy explained, "Dr. Theodore Veritas is a friend of ours. And, yes, he has a great name—first and last. But after years of brainwashing at the 'best' colleges and universities, it's hard for him to give up his faith in the big bang and evolution. However, he is a gifted scientist, and he does have a nice museum.

"Well," Billy continued, "since it's getting late, how about we just go over to the library as our first information source. We can gather some books for you to take home and look through. Now, which library is on Ms. Lution's list?"

David looked back at the list and groaned. "I should have guessed. It's *The Library of Secular Science*. That's the library founded by Ms. Lution's father, Dr. Edward Lution—Ph.D. times three. When it opened last year, Dr. Lution gave a big speech about 'cutting no cost to make the most up-to-date *scientific knowledge* available to all the people of Greenville.' If you think Ms. Lution's big on evolution, you should meet her dad!"

"Well," Billy said, "I guess we'll just have to go and check it out for ourselves."

****

Inside the library, everything was quiet. With its glass ceiling and nice furnishings, it was bright and inviting. But, after scanning the evolutionary posters on the walls, Abel turned to Darin and whispered, "Cap'n, I sense danger."

Darin nodded. "Yeah, Scotty. Set your phaser on stun."

"Well," Billy chuckled, "this isn't my kind of library, either. But we do need a few good books on why so many scientists believe in the big bang." Turning to David, he said, "Always remember, you can't refute evolutionists' conclusions without seeing what they believe and why they believe it. If your report is going to be *scientific*, you're going to have to look at *both* sides."

After looking around, the newly formed Creation Science Club started over toward some computers along one wall. "Hey," David whispered, "there's Jack and Jill Hill. They're in my honors science class. They must be working on their reports, too. Look at the cool videos they have up on their screens!"

David moved forward quickly. "Hey, Jack. Hey, Jill. Whatcha lookin' at?"

"Man, David!" Jack whispered excitedly. "You should see everything we've found out already. These computers are so cool!"

"Yeah!" Jill jumped in. "It's like all you do is type in *evolution*, and everything you need is right there: News reports, TV clips, and all kinds of interviews with smart scientists."

"I just watched the neatest clip on the big bang," Jack said.

"And I'm listening to this scientist explain how they know that the universe is 14.5 billion years old." Jill added, "It's everything you need." Then she smiled at David and pointed to the computer next to her. "You can use this computer, it's open."

As Billy went off to look up a few books on the evolutionists' view of the origin of the universe, David joined his friends. "This is gonna make everything so easy. All I should have to do is type in the word *creation* to find all the information I need."

Everyone leaned forward to watch as David typed in the word *creation* on his screen. David read aloud the small definition that came up. "*Creation* is a word commonly used to describe the universe, the earth, and all that is in them. This term comes from the old-fashioned religious belief that the earth was 'created' by a god in six days." David's voice dropped as he continued, "To research the *religious* understanding of *creation*, type in *mythology*. To research the *scientific* understanding of origins, type in *evolution*."

Jill giggled at what he had read. David blushed and slouched down in his chair, discouraged.

Jack shushed Jill, then said to David, "Hey, man, don't feel bad. My uncle says a lot of people are still confused about all that stuff. You know, my uncle's a scientist over at Quantum Leap University. He knows *everything*. We're going to visit his lab as our third information source. You can come, too, if you want."

"Thanks," David said in a small voice. "I'll let you know. Anyway, I guess I'd better get home now. Ummm...see you guys at school." Then David went toward the exit without looking back.

Darin and Abel followed behind David. "So, Scotty," Darin asked, "who beams us up to the ship when you're part of the landing party?"

Abel thought for a minute, then answered, "Well, I guess that depends on who David is. If he's Mr. Sulu, then Mr. Chekov will have to beam us up. But if he's Chekov, then Sulu will have to do it." Abel stopped short when he saw David hop right into the jeep. "Well, would ya look at that!" he said. "He just beamed himself onto the Enterprise without contacting anyone."

David couldn't help but smile a bit at the twins' expressions of stunned shock. "I'm Mr. Spock," he announced. "And, I never leave the ship without my own self-teleporting gizmo."

"Self-teleporting gizmo?" Captain Kirk questioned. "Is that Federation certified?"

"Nope," Mr. Spock answered in a very non-Vulcan manner. "But y'all can use it if ya like."

"Oh, oh, oh," Scotty raised his hand. "Me first! Let me use it first!"

"No way!" Captain Kirk pushed Scotty's hand down. "I'm the captain. I get first dibs."

"You best be careful, Cap'n," the engineer cautioned. "You be forgettin' about me Scottish temper."

"Oh, blow it out your Scottish nose," Captain Kirk said, as he lunged at Scotty.

David laughed while the two battled it out until Billy came and ordered, "Everyone get in. We've got to get David home." Then he turned to David. "Here, I found some books I think will help with your research."

David's smile faded. "Thanks," he mumbled, then shoved the books into his backpack without looking at them.

As Billy drove along the country roads, David just watched the fields go by without saying anything. Finally,

Darin reached over and tapped David on the shoulder. "Uh...a penny for your thoughts, David-dude."

Abel gave Darin a shove and said, "I think you'd better offer him some serious money—it looks like he's having some serious thoughts."

David tried to smile, then sighed. "Jill thinks I'm silly. I mean, it doesn't seem fair. Here I am tryin' to stand up for what the Bible says, and people keep knockin' me down. I just don't understand why everybody seems to think that God is so...*unscientific*."

As Billy pulled into David's driveway, he turned to him and answered. "They think that way because that's just what the devil wants them to think. We must never forget the spiritual side of things."

David looked away. "Ms. Lution says evolution has no *spiritual side*."

"Yep," Abel nodded emphatically. "That's totally all the way true. Evolution has no spiritual side. It insists on being all-natural. It wants no God, no religion."

David shook his head. "Ms. Lution says that *science* has no *spiritual side*—no God, no religion."

Darin leaned forward. "Whoa, dude. Now, that's way off. Science is a gift from God. It's through science that we discover, learn, go forward, and grow. It's dumb-old evolution that's trying to shut off our brains and turn us into well-dressed monkeys."

Billy joined back in. "You see, David, the problems all start when people try to separate science from God. But you just can't separate creation from the Creator. And you can't separate the laws of nature from the Maker of those laws."

"So, why can't a Christian just believe God used evolution to create everything?"

Billy looked solemn. "A Christian *can* believe in evolution. Many very real, good Christian folks believe what they've been taught about evolution. However, confusion starts sprouting up when these believers see that evolution and the Bible just don't seem to match up. Pretty soon, these sincere folks start having to make excuses for what's written in the Bible. And that can't be right. God is absolute. His Word is true. Science has to fit into God's Word, not the other way around."

Billy handed David his backpack, and added, "Remember, David, this is a *real* battle against a *real* giant that wants to turn people away from the truth of God's Word."

David nodded his head thoughtfully. "You're right—this *is* a battle. And my dad always says our best weapon is prayer. You can bet that I'll be praying about this one."

CHAPTER 3

On Saturday at noon, Darin, Abel, and David all sat groaning in their booth at Biggie Burgers.

"Well, David," Billy said, shaking his head in disbelief, "you ate three of Mr. Biggie's biggest burgers. I didn't think anyone could out-eat the T-twins!"

Darin was holding his stomach, unable to speak.

David managed a smile. "My Papa always says, 'We may be small, but no one can out-eat an Avila.'"

Abel sat up, burped four nice big ones, then managed to get out, "A rematch…we demand a rematch."

Billy stood up to throw the trash away. "Well, none of you are in any kind of shape to try a rematch right now. In fact, I don't think you're in any kind of shape to do anything but sprawl out on a couple of picnic tables at the park. So, let's head on out to Green Trees and take a half hour digestive break before we drive over to Dr. Teddy's museum.

****

At the park, Abel and Darin squabbled briefly over who got the table with the most shade. Darin won and immediately fell flat on his back on the tabletop. Abel grumbled a bit, then fell flat on his back on the next closest table.

"Go ahead and lie down," Billy told David. "I'll keep guard."

"No thanks. I think if I take any position that's not vertical, I'll lose my lunch. But…I did have a question for you."

Billy walked over a little ways to the nearest bench and sat down. "Ask away," he said, crossing his legs and leaning back.

"Well…I know that Darin and Abel have Asperger Syndrome. But…what does that really mean?"

Billy stretched his back. "Boy, that's a tough question, with no cut and dried answers. First of all, you have to understand that those who have Asperger's see the world differently than your "average Joe." It's not their fault, that's just the way it is. Now, from the medical standpoint, doctors consider AS to be a part of the broader Autism Spectrum—it's grouped together with autism and Tourette Syndrome. Some doctors even widen the autism family to include ADD and ADHD."

"I have a cousin with autism," David said. "She lives in Guatemala. But she doesn't talk much at all. And, you know, the T-twins don't seem to ever stop talking."

Billy had to laugh. "You're right about that."

After a pause, Billy continued, "Well, Asperger's and autism do have several things in common. However, they also have many significant differences."

"Yeah, like I said, my cousin hardly ever talks. A lot of times she just screams. And, she's, like…you know…slow. But, Darin and Abel are way super-smart."

"Well, that's why it's called a *spectrum disorder*." Billy turned on his bench and used his finger to trace an arch on the picnic table. "Think of it as a rainbow. You see, a rainbow has several different colors—red, orange, yellow, green, blue, and purple. These colors could stand for ADD, ADHD, Tourette's, Asperger's and autism.

"But look again at the rainbow—each color actually has countless shades within itself. It's the same with the Autism Spectrum. One person with ADD can be quite different from another person with ADD. And someone with Asperger's can be very different from someone else with Asperger's. They're different, but the same *color*.

"But then, look back at the whole rainbow—each color just kinda blends into the next. That's how it is with the different disorders in the Autism Spectrum—they're different, but all related."

David stared at Billy's invisible drawing with a perplexed look. "Wow, I guess I kinda understand...maybe."

Billy chuckled. "It's a lot to try to take in. For now, let's just think about Asperger Syndrome. Okay, first of all, boys are a lot more likely to have AS than girls. Second, those with AS often have a higher than average intelligence, sometimes much higher than average—like the T-twins. They generally focus intensely on just a few subjects, and excel in those subjects.

"The drawback is that these added smarts seem to come with a loss of social skills. Aspies often have a difficult time understanding what others expect of them. Reading people's facial expressions and body language doesn't come naturally for them. On top of this, they seem to only be able to see things from one perspective—their own. So, they continually clash with 'regular' folks. This makes people uncomfortable and frustrated. But, the person with AS is left wondering why the other people are getting upset."

"So, then, how come Darin and Abel seem to get along with people so well?"

"The twins' parents worked hard, in a loving and patient way, to teach them how to…well, I guess, communicate better. You could say it's like Darin and Abel were born speaking Spanish. So, their parents taught them English. I mean, 'Spanish' will always be their native language. But with encouragement, they are always getting more fluent with their 'English.'"

Noticing the twins starting to stir, David asked quickly, "How come Darin and Abel hang out with you all the time? I mean, where's their mom and dad?"

Billy stood up. "The boys' dad was a very good man. But he died of cancer when they were 13. Their mom is a good woman, but has to work 9 to 5 since their dad died. She moved out here close to Greenville a few years back. Carmen and I met her at church when the boys were 14. And, since we don't have any children of our own, we decided we could be sort of a second family to the boys. Besides, they're excellent assistants for all the research I have to do."

"Anyway," David said, "I'm really glad I can hang around with you guys."

"And, we're mighty glad to have you. It's good for the boys to have a friend like you. Even though they're three years older than you, emotionally they're closer to your age. So actually, by spending time with you, they're learning by example what society expects from teenagers."

Darin and Abel were now walking sluggishly toward them. "I feel like I was run over by a truck," Darin complained.

Billy shook his head at the boys' hair sticking out every which direction. "You look like you were run over by a truck. But I think you'll feel better once we get moving." He looked at their hair again. "Though I doubt you'll look much better."

****

After Billy parked the jeep, David hopped out and read the big sign in front of the museum. "*The Museum of Certain Science.*"

Abel and Darin snickered and winked at each other. "Or *The Museum of UNcertain Science*, as we like to call it."

"Why would you call it *The Museum of UNcertain Science*?" David asked.

"You'll see..." Billy laughed as he opened the front door and let them all file in.

David took a minute to glance around the large front room, then exclaimed, "Man! Dr. Veritas sure has some pretty cool stuff here."

Engineer Scott grabbed David by the arm. "Aye, Mr. Spock, sir, you must come and see the grandest place of all—the astronomy room. Space...the final frontier. All we need is Dr. Veritas to give us a private tour."

Out of the shadows came a man with a long nose, a small beard, and glasses. "Well, well, Billy, my friend," he said shaking Billy's hand. "Who has your gang brought along with you to examine these great halls of *certain science*?"

Billy put his hand on David's shoulder and introduced his friends to each other. "David, this is Dr. Teddy Veritas. Teddy, this is David Avila. We've teamed up with David to research and write a science report on the origin of the universe."

"I'm glad to meet you, David," Dr. Veritas said. "You must be part of Ms. Eva Lution's honors science class. I would be happy to give you a tour of our spectacular space room and answer any questions you might have."

Darin and Abel met each other in the air with a double high-five and started to run toward the astronomy room. Dr. Veritas, however, stepped in front of them and said calmly, "David's ticket is on the house, but you others will need to purchase your tickets over at the booth." Then he led David away.

Darin complained, "I don't know if I want to use my money to support *this* kind of science."

"I understand," Billy said, as they crossed over to the ticket booth. "But you two need to remember our prayer—that someday Dr. Teddy will be on our side of the battle, and that this museum will be used for God's glory. You never know, God can do anything."

Suddenly, a head peeked out from behind the ticket booth. "Hey!" a nice-looking man announced, "you must be Christians. I'm a Christian, too. My name's Cliff—Cliff Newman."

After introductions, Cliff continued, "Man, you were right when you said that God can do anything. I was certainly heading the wrong way fast during my college days. I thought I knew it all and was in total control. Then, one night, *Boom!*—a sleepy semi driver crushed my car. I mean it was totally smashed. Amazingly, I walked away with only a few bruises. At that moment, I knew one thing—it could've only been God who had saved my life. So, I gave my life to Him."

"Praise the Lord!" Billy said. "What a wonderful testimony of God's grace in your life."

"Yeah," Cliff said. "After the accident, my eyes seemed to open up to God at work in everything—especially nature. First, for several years, I just kinda hiked around the world and *soaked up* everything God made. Then, I went back to school to be a park ranger. I've even applied to be a ranger at the Grand Canyon."

Billy smiled. "Nature certainly does testify to the awesome power of God."

"Yeah," Cliff nodded. "It sure does show the power of God. I mean, just think, only an amazing and powerful God could take a tiny dot, blow it up in the big bang, and then orchestrate everything just right so that it evolved over billions of years into something so exactly perfect and beautiful."

"Well, ya know, Cliff-man," Darin said, "actually, the Bible doesn't really talk about a *big bang* or about *millions and billions of years* or anything about *evolution*."

"Well," Cliff looked thoughtful for a moment. "I guess God must have just left some of those *details* out. It had to have happened that way. I mean, I studied all about it over at Quantum Leap University."

Abel joined in. "Hey, ya know, think about this. Who was there in the beginning? God or those evolutionists? And what do you think? Did God give us the Bible to teach us, or to confuse us? I mean, we're scientists and we believe that God writes clearly and means just what he says. It's men who weren't there who are trying to explain the universe without a creator—without God."

"Hmmm..." Cliff said in confusion, "that sounds pretty radical. I don't know..."

Billy smiled and said, "No worries. We'll just say one more thing. Read the Bible—especially Genesis. The God who saved you in that terrible car crash wrote the Bible. You can trust what He says."

"Well, what have you gentlemen been doing?" Dr. Teddy's voice rang out. "You haven't even purchased your tickets yet, and we've seen the entire universe." Dr. Veritas looked down at David and continued, "David, here, has a quick mind, and asked lots of good questions. I must admit that some of them, ummm, caught me a bit unprepared."

Back in the jeep, David laughed. "I see now why you guys call *it The Museum of UNcertain Science*. I asked Dr. Veritas if there was any solid evidence that really proved the big bang. He just stroked his beard and said, 'Hmmm...I'm not really certain how to answer that.' Then, I asked him where the small bit of matter that exploded into the universe came from in the first place. And he just tapped his nose and said, 'Ummm, we're uncertain about that...'"

David had been doing a very good imitation of Dr. Veritas's voice and gestures, so everyone had to join him in a hearty laugh. It was a happy group of creation scientists that drove through Greenville back toward David's house.

When Billy finally pulled into the driveway, David hopped out of the jeep and said, "Don't forget, on Tuesday I'm going with my parents to visit an old lawyer friend of theirs as my third information source. But I'll come up to your place on Thursday so we can finish things up for this report."

****

That Thursday, David joined the CSC up on Maple Hill. Darin and Abel had the cabin door locked and whispered for Billy to keep David busy for a while. So, Billy grabbed his gun and led David further up the hill behind the cabin. "Look there!" he pointed. "Those tracks belong to Mr. Big. Or maybe I should say, *Mrs.* Big. She's that tricky black bear that seemed to think you smelled like a good lunch—the biggest sow-bear I've ever seen. She keeps showing up in our surveillance videos, but never ends up in the twins' trap."

David followed as Billy traced the bear's trail up to a rocky area on the hill. There they lost the tracks. While Billy studied the ground to the north, David looked for some tracks going east. Pushing away some underbrush, David found a deep, fresh print. He turned toward Billy and called in a whisper, "Hey, look what I found!" But it wasn't Billy who answered. Out of the nearby brush Mrs. Big rose up with a huffing growl. Her eyes locked on David. Every hair on his body stood straight up and tried to run, but his legs wouldn't budge. He couldn't move.

Billy, however, was all action. In a flash he had his rifle up on his shoulder. *Bang!* The bear dropped down onto all fours. *Bang*! It jumped back and turned to run further up into the woods.

David let out a long, shaky breath. "Did you hit her? Is she going to die?"

Billy lowered the gun. "Naw, I had to shoot high since I thought you might decide to run. And I sure didn't want you runnin' right into one of my bullets.

"But, I guess I'll have to call a deputy out here after all. He's got some dogs and can down her with a tranquilizer dart and relocate her. We can't have her denning around here, since she's sure to have cubs over the winter. And, no way do we want a big, grumpy mama bear around here come spring. No way."

David wiped his nose to make sure no adrenaline was dripping out, then agreed, "No way."

****

Back at the cabin, Darin, Abel, and Mrs. James were waiting with concerned looks on their faces. "No worries," Billy waved to them. "No one's hurt! Mrs. Big just got a little too close for comfort."

Mrs. James looked relieved and headed back into the cabin, but Darin and Abel ran over to them with a draft of David's report in hand.

"Wow, David-dude!" Darin said, "this is great—fantazgreat! You wrote like a real pro!" They handed the report to Billy and whispered, "We need a little more time. Mrs. Carmen is just putting on the finishing touches." Then they ran giggling back to the cabin.

Billy leaned against a tree and began flipping through the notes David had gathered from his meeting with Mr. Brown. "Wow!" Billy said. "I like the notes you took. This old attorney certainly has a Christ-like mind. I'd love to meet him."

David smiled and said, "It sure was encouraging to talk with a Bible-believing man, especially after visiting *The Library of Secular Science* and *The Museum of UNcertain Science*."

But, even as he spoke, David's smile started to fade, and his eyebrows drew together into a thoughtful frown.

Billy watched the excitement seem to drain out of David. "Hey, what's the matter?"

Looking down toward the creek, David sighed. "Well, in some ways I feel like I've learned so much, and have a lot to say. But…I guess I can still hear Ms. Lution saying, 'David, you have a right to your religious beliefs. However, evolution is *science*. Faith in a Creator is *not* scientific, it's just a belief.'"

Billy put down the report and stood up. "If you've learned one thing in these past couple of weeks, it's that evolution is just as much a *belief about the past* as creation."

"Yeah, I know," David said, kicking a stone down the hill. "Creationists *believe* the universe came from a Creator, and evolutionists *believe* it came from a natural cause—the big bang." He walked down to the rock he had kicked and kicked it again, with Billy following. "The problem is, Ms. Lution is going to say, 'Evolution is science because evolutionists use evidence, observation and logic to come to their conclusions.' Then she'll say, 'Believing the Bible's account of a creator is just *blind* faith—*not* science.'"

Picking his own rock to kick, Billy aimed and landed it in the creek. "It's tough," he acknowledged. "The first day we met Ms. Lution, she pulled that one on me. Evolutionists love to say that anyone who believes creation can't be a real scientist." Sinking another rock into the creek, he continued. "It seems like they just close their eyes and stop up their ears to all the honest-to-goodness *science* behind the research we do."

David aimed and sent his own rock into the thin trickle of water wandering through the creek bed. "Billy, I see you guys doing experiments all the time. But I need a simple, every-day example of *creation* being *scientific*."

Billy smiled and bent down. "Hey, look at this rock. It's shaped just like a cowboy boot." Then, he picked up another rock. "And look at this one. If you look at it right, it looks kinda like that mean ol' bear's head."

David jumped down into the creek bed. "Look, here's one that looks like a kangaroo."

Billy took the rock David had and held it in his hand. "Now, how do you suppose this rock got like this?"

David shrugged. "Just erosion, I guess."

Billy nodded. "How'd you know that?"

David shrugged again. "It just seems obvious. I mean, it was right here in the creek. Must have had a lot of water flowing over it. All the edges are smoothed like they get when they've been bumping along with the water."

As he continued looking among the rocks, Billy agreed. "Sounds like a real *scientific* conclusion. You used evidence, observation, and logic to come up with that answer."

Suddenly, David pounced on something. "Check it out!" he whooped. "I found a real authentic arrowhead! Darin said he's found some down here. And I've looked before, but never found any. I can't wait to show him."

Billy examined the flint stone in David's hand. "Hmmm..." he said doubtfully. "What makes you so sure that's an arrowhead?"

"Come on, Billy," David laughed. "It's obvious!"

"So," Billy said, scratching his chin thoughtfully, "are you telling me that you think some Native American, whom you've never seen, chipped this flint to this specific shape for a predetermined purpose? How could you know that?"

David caught on to Billy's point. "Well," he answered, "evidence, observation, and logic all point to this arrowhead being made by an unseen, intelligent creator for a purpose."

"Exactly!" Billy slapped David on the back, then wrapped up his point. "So, evidence, observation, and logic can be used to determine that nature created the kangaroo rock. *And*, evidence, observation, and logic can be used to determine that an intelligent being created the arrowhead with a specific purpose in mind."

"So," David smiled in triumph, "both conclusions are equally *scientific!"*

****

Back up the hill, Billy and David sat down and continued looking through the draft of David's report and his notes. "Man," David said, "now I remember Mr. Brown saying that some of creation's best evidence is found right in the Bible itself. It's like God knew some day people would reject Him as the Creator. So, He put all the proof we needed right in the Bible."

Billy pointed to a section in David's notes. "Look here! Mr. Brown said it well when he said, 'Time and Chance is the devil's lie.' It really is deception that intelligent people put so much time, effort, and money into trying to prove the big bang and evolution, while totally rejecting all the evidence that supports creation."

"Well," David said, "I guess it's just like you said when we started this report—it's a spiritual battle. I mean, right before I met you guys, things were really hard. It was like evolution was chasing me. It was right there ready to get me. I felt like the only thing I could do was give up and lock myself in a cage.

"But now, I feel like David with his sling and stones. It's like I finally have something to fight with. I feel ready to meet and defeat the Giant of Deception. I want to win back God's glory as the Creator."

"Amen, David! That's just what we want to see happen through all your science reports this year."

At that moment, Darin and Abel appeared at the cabin door, with Mrs. James smiling behind them. *"Surprise!"* they shouted.

"Look, David-dude," Darin explained, "Abel and I—uh, with a little help from Mrs. Carmen—made you our famous four-layer-four-flavor-four-pound-cake to celebrate the completion of your first report. But," Darin added, as he set the cake down on a flat tree stump, "this isn't only a celebration—it's also a challenge."

"Ah," David said kneeling beside the stump, "a cake-eating contest! You guys are pretty brave after the stomping I gave you at Biggie Burgers."

"Ha-ha," Darin said in a very serious tone. "You'd better just prepare yourself for a major-blast-tastic defeat. For, I'm telling you, *no one* can eat more cake than I can."

"Humph!" Scotty snorted through Abel as he took his place by the cake. "The Cap'n, here, has always been a wee bit over confident in his abilities. He might have warp-power cake eating abilities, but I myself am equipped with the latest trans-warp eating engines."

David fixed his eyes on the cake. "I wouldn't concern yourself with the Captain if I were you, Mr. Scott. It's the Vulcan that's gonna leave you in his dust."

"Okay, you guys," Billy said taking out his stopwatch. "Stop your braggin' and get ready to prove yourselves."

All three boys picked up their forks.

Billy winked at Mrs. Carmen and said, "You made the cake, you start the party."

"All right," Mrs. James smiled. "The winner is the one who can eat the most cake in the next 60 seconds. On your mark! Get set! Go!"

CHAPTER 4

The Origin of the Universe
(God the Creator)

by David J. Avila

Introduction

The latest scientific ideas concerning the origin of the universe show that there are two *very different* theories. Evolutionists would like us to see the debate between these two theories as a battle between science and religion. They present their big bang theory as a scientific fact, but creation as an unscientific belief. In this way, evolutionists try to put creation in a category outside of science.

In reality, the big bang and creation start out on equal footing. They both start with one huge fact—the existence of the universe. And just as importantly, they both have all the same evidence to observe. However, these two theories come to very different conclusions. This is because each theory begins with a very different assumption (foundational belief) about the origin of the universe, and then tries to interpret (make sense out of) the evidence.

Evolution begins with the assumption that everything has a "natural" cause and can be explained without God. Based on this assumption, evolution claims the *big bang* as the origin of the universe. *Creation* begins with the assumption that the Bible is true. And the Bible says that God is the Maker of the universe. A true scientist will look closely at both theories (beliefs) to see which one explains the evidence better.

For this report, I will first show the difference between operational science and historical science. I will show that the big bang and creation are *both* historical science. Then I will look at how both theories explain the existing evidence. Finally, I will show that the evidence makes better sense when we begin with what the Bible says, with the eyewitness account of God the Creator.

Operational and Historical Science

Operational Science deals with things that are *observable, testable,* and *repeatable.* For example, a scientist might *observe* different objects falling to the ground. After some thought, he comes up with the theory that objects of any mass will fall to the ground at the same rate. So, he *tests* his theory by dropping two different objects off a tall tower and *observes* them hitting the ground at the same time. Then, he *tests* his theory under different conditions. Finally, other scientists *repeat* his experiment and consistently reach the same conclusions—objects of any mass will fall to the ground at the same time. Years later, his experiment is even *repeated* on the moon as an astronaut drops a hammer and a feather—and the whole world *observes* them hitting the ground at the same time.

This kind of operational science (observable, testable, and repeatable) has benefited us in many ways—paving the way for the discovery of medicines and vaccines, and leading to astounding technological inventions like the computer to type our reports and even rockets that take us to the moon.

Historical Science differs greatly from operational science because it deals with things that happened in the past. These things are *not* observable and *cannot* be tested or repeated. The origin of the universe is historical science—no human being observed it being formed, and it certainly cannot be tested or repeated in a lab. A theory of the origin of the universe begins with a belief about how the universe might have formed. It then tries to fit the present observable evidence into that theory.

Evolution's big bang and biblical creation are both historical science. Neither theory can be observed, tested, or repeated. Both theories *begin with a belief* about the origin of the universe and then try to *explain the evidence* using that belief. In looking at both theories, a scientist must objectively consider which one explains the evidence *better*.

The Big Bang

The idea of the big bang began after a famous scientist, Edwin Hubble, observed that distant galaxies have a 'red-shift.' Most scientists agree that this redshift shows that the universe is expanding. The redshift is an observable fact—*the evidence.* To explain this evidence, evolution claims that about 15 billion years ago, a really hot, dense, tiny dot exploded, forming the universe and everything that we see today. But, this is not operational science. No human being observed it, and it can't be tested or repeated. The big bang is historical science—a *belief* trying to explain the evidence—the redshift.

However, the big bang does not really explain the evidence well. It leaves many important questions unanswered. The big bang does not answer *why* or even *how* the universe began. It gives no explanation as to where the tiny dot came from in the first place. It seems to tell us *everything* just came from *nothing*, and that order came from a chaotic explosion. How did stars form? How did galaxies form? How did our solar system form? How did the earth form? How did life on earth begin? *None* of these questions are answered.

Some evolutionists claim that the big bang is in agreement with all the evidence that we see today. But it actually *contradicts* much of the evidence. According to the big bang, the universe has no center and no edge, but observed redshifts seem to show that it has both a center and an edge. Also, the big bang predicts that matter should be spread evenly throughout space, but the Hubble Space Telescope shows just the opposite—that galaxies are grouped together, leaving large areas of empty space.

So, a scientist can *choose to believe* the big bang as the origin of the universe, but it just doesn't explain the evidence well and it leaves many questions unanswered.

The Creator God

Creation is also historical science. However, creation science does claim to have a written account of the origin of the universe from an actual eyewitness—God the Creator. According to the Bible, "[God] made the heavens, even the highest heavens, and all their starry host, the earth and all that is on it, the seas and all that is in them. [He gives] life to everything, and the multitudes of heaven worship [him]" (Nehemiah 9:6). "For by him all things were created: things in heaven and on earth, visible and invisible...all things were created by him and for him" (Colossians 1:16). "By faith we understand that the universe was formed at God's command" (Hebrews 11:3).

But, does creation really explain the evidence? The founders of operational science believed that the universe was made by a rational Creator and that it would, therefore, be rational and orderly. This is exactly what they found to be true. This confirmed their belief in a Creator/Designer. "The heavens declare the glory of God; the skies proclaim the work of his hands" (Psalm 19:1).

But what about other scientific evidence, like the redshift and an expanding universe? And what about a universe with a center and an edge, and galaxies grouped together leaving large areas of empty space? How do these fit in with creation?

One creation scientist has worked out a new theory that explains the redshift. This theory is also in agreement with the evidence showing that the universe has a center and an edge. Applying Einstein's theory of relativity, this theory explains how stars millions of light years away can be seen even though they were created only thousands of years ago. So, there is no need to invent billions of years. Finally, this theory does *not* reject a Creator as unscientific. Instead, it is founded on the belief that a rational Creator made an orderly universe with a plan and with a purpose.

Conclusion

The formation of the universe is not observable, testable, or repeatable. Therefore, the two main theories of the origin of the universe are both historical science. Both must begin with a *belief* about the origin of the universe and then try to explain the evidence.

Evolution's big bang begins with the belief that the origin of the universe has a *natural* cause and that a *creator* is not necessary. Creation begins with the belief that the Bible is true, that God exists, and that He created the heavens and the earth. So, the question is, which theory explains the evidence better?

We observe matter, energy, and order in our universe. We see our solar system running like clockwork. We find the earth filled with all kinds of living things. Does this evidence suggest that the universe and everything in it randomly came from *nothing*, with no purpose or meaning? Or does the evidence point to a Creator, who formed it all for a specific purpose?

"The heavens declare the glory of God; the skies proclaim the work of his hands" (Psalm 19:1). The evidence makes better sense when we begin with what the Bible says, with the eyewitness account of—God the Creator.

****

After grading David's report, Ms. Lution decided to go and have a talk with her father, the founder of The Lution Evolution Foundation.

"So, Dad," Ms. Lution said a bit nervously, "have you ever really read the Bible?"

"What!" Dr. Lution ejected. "Why on earth would I waste my time reading through such a long and tedious book of fairy tales?"

"Well," Eva sat up a bit straighter, "one of my students claims that evolution's big bang is really just a *belief*, the same as creation. He said that, 'A *true* scientist must look closely at both theories to see which one explains the evidence better.'"

Dr. Lution frowned and told his daughter sternly, "That's nonsense. Evolution is science, dealing with the facts of nature. The Bible is nothing but a bunch of ancient stories—old-fashioned superstitions.

Ms. Lution bristled, "Mom was a geologist—a scientist, yet she read the Bible and prayed with me every night."

"That's just the way she was raised," her dad answered shortly. "Besides, what do you remember? Your mother died before you turned seven." Dr. Lution looked both angry and sad as he continued. "There is no *Creator God*. Life is nothing more than survival of the fittest. Natural selection may pick and choose heartlessly, but it eventually leads to a better, more adapted species."

"But Dad," Eva softened her tone, "aren't you just *choosing* to believe evolution without looking at the other side of the issue?"

"There is no other side to science!"

"That's no different than what we accuse the creationists of doing."

Dr. Lution sighed and asked, "Eva, where are you heading with this?"

"Well," she answered, "you know I've never believed anything coming from the creationists. But then again," she admitted with a smile, "I guess I've never taken them seriously enough to look into their crazy ideas. Maybe to be a *true* scientist, I need to take some time to look into what the creationists have to say."

"You'd make much better use of your time by finally finishing your Ph.D."

Eva Lution stood up and walked toward the door. "I've spent plenty of time on *our* side of the issue." Slipping into her jacket, she looked at her scowling father. "David said the Bible is loaded with evidence that backs up creation. I find that very hard to believe. But how can I refute it if I don't take the time to see for myself what the Bible, and those creationists, have to say."

Dr. Lution jumped up and slapped his hand on the table. "You're wasting your time. Listen to me, and just leave the Bible where it belongs—in the past."

Eva tightened her lips and answered, "Dad, you're treating me like a child. It's not like looking at what the Bible has to say is going to turn me into some sort of hallelujah-shouting televangelist." With that, she left, shutting the door firmly behind her.

PART 2

The Age of the Earth

CHAPTER 5

Early on a beautiful fall morning, Billy James smiled to himself as he drove his jeep across Rocky Creek Bridge and up into the trees of Maple Hill. In a carefree, pleasant voice, he sang:

> "All creatures of our God and King,
> Ladybugs lift your voice and sing,
> Oh, praise him, Alleluia.
> Inchworms and butterflies rejoice,
> Bluebirds and finches fly your course,
> Oh, praise him, monkeys praise him,
> Alleluia, bunnies praise him!"

Pulling to a stop, he parked in front of the Maple Hill cabin—now also known as the Creation Science Club cabin. Hopping out of his jeep, he stopped to listen to the birds singing their familiar morning songs. Suddenly, an unfamiliar call floated down the hill to him. He pulled his eyebrows down in a puzzled expression, and headed toward the cabin.

"Hey, Darin!" Billy called as soon as he stepped into the cabin. "Hey, Darin, Quick! Where are the binoculars? I heard some strange new bird a ways up in the woods! Darin! Where are you?"

Billy rounded the corner and nearly ran Abel over. "Whoa! Sorry, Abel. Have you seen Darin?"

Abel shook his head. "Nope. He wasn't with us when Mom brought me over on her way to work. He stayed up late working on some gadget, and then was gone before we even woke up this morning."

"Well," Billy said, "we'll call his cell in a minute. First—I heard some strange bird back in the woods. It sounded like this—*Heee-yelp, heee-yelp*."

"Hmmm…I know the calls of about 150 different birds. The closest that comes to is a peacock."

Billy said, "Nah. *I* know what a peacock sounds like. This *wasn't* a peacock."

"Heee-yelp, heee-yelp!" the distant but clear call came through the woods.

"There it is again!" Billy ran to the window. "I wish I had the binoculars."

"Shucks!" Abel said. "Who needs binoculars? I've been reading up on how to stalk up *real* close to live biological specimens for on-field, non-disruptive observation."

Billy smiled. "Well then, let's go!" They both took off running in the direction of the strange call.

After a few minutes, Abel slowed to a walk. He had Billy move forward with him slowly—step by step. Then, they stopped.

"Shhh," Abel whispered. "Look. I see something way up in that tall tree ahead. Boy, it's big. It's…" Suddenly, Abel started running toward the tree.

Billy sprinted after him, calling in a hushed voice, "Wait, Abel, don't scare it away."

"Don't worry," Abel shouted with a chuckle. "It's already so scared it can't move. Your mystery bird is very rare. In fact, it's one of a kind—the crazy *Darin-bird.*"

"You mean," Billy said, stopping for a breath, "that's Darin way up there?" Then he busted out laughing. "I should have known. He's not saying *Heee-yelp*, he's saying *Help!"*

High up in the tree, Darin heard Billy's booming laugh. "Heee-yelp! I'm over here, stuck in this tree. I dropped my climbing gear and I can't get down."

"Don't worry, little Darin-bird," Billy called up. "Hang tight while I run back and get *my* gear. Then we'll have you down in a jiffy."

A little while later, when everyone was safe on the ground, Darin was flapping around Billy as he explained excitedly, "I was testing out my new *bionic binoculars*, and..."

"Hey," Abel jumped in, "I thought you gave up on those for good."

"Well, I did kinda sorta kinda did. But then, last night, in a state of minor sleep deprivation, I entered into the *total genius zone*."

"No way!" Abel said. "That's your third time and I've only been there once."

Darin did a bit of a strut, but then continued. "Anyway, I got them to work. You won't believe it! Talk about totally awesome bionics! I could actually tell the time on the Greenville Church clock! It said twelve minutes after six."

"No way!" Billy said. "It was dark at twelve minutes after six."

"That's just it!" Darin strutted some more. "I had to test my bionic binoculars for all conditions, including night vision, to make sure they'd work for our trip to the Grand Canyon. Just wait till you see 'em in action—you'll be so impressed."

"I'm already impressed," Billy replied. "But, from now on, Darin-bird, I want you to learn a lesson from the real peacocks and stay a little closer to the ground!"

As they headed back to the cabin, Abel leaned eagerly toward his brother. "So, how'd you do it? How'd you make 'em work?"

Darin glanced at Billy, then put a finger to his lips. "Shhh, I don't want Billy to know that I really don't have a clue how I got 'em to work."

****

It was Saturday morning at the Avila home. David was just finishing breakfast with his family. David's dad smiled at him and said, "I'm glad the Creation Science Club is able to help you out on this second science report. It sounds like you had a good trip over to QLU yesterday. We'll be praying this report can help bring the glory of creation back to God, just like your first one did."

David's older sister, Corina, smirked a bit. "They're a pretty strange group if you ask me."

Mr. Avila gave her a warning look, but said pleasantly, "Not everybody fits into the same mold. God makes everyone unique."

"Well," she agreed, "Abel and Darin sure are *unique*."

David stopped eating his eggs and said defensively, "Abel and Darin have Asperger Syndrome. They can't help it. Besides, they're way smarter than you, and I think they're lots of fun."

Cory looked a bit ashamed. "Hey, I didn't know they had whatever-it-is-you-said-they-had. What is that anyway?"

David paused to try to come up with a concise explanation. "Well, Billy says it's related to autism, but a lot different. Asperger Syndrome itself can come out different in different people. However, the main symptoms are a higher than average intelligence, but a lack of regularly-accepted social skills. They have the tendency to hyper-zoom-in on just a few subjects that they find interesting."

"Well, I do think they're nice and all." Cory smiled. "I guess I just didn't understand why they kinda act like little kids when they're so smart."

David shrugged. "They're just having fun. They don't have the usual teenage 'need' to act cool. So, instead, they just do what's fun, even if it might look silly to other people."

Mr. Avila spoke up. "I wish more teenagers could just be themselves and have innocent fun instead of trying to impress everyone with some tough-guy act."

Just then, they heard three short beeps of a horn from outside. Mrs. Avila smiled and said, "There's Mr. James and the twins now. David, don't forget the lunch I packed for you all." Then, after an affectionate farewell, David raced out the door to the waiting jeep. He hopped in, buckled up, and they were on their way.

At *The Library of Secular Science*, the CSC sat out in the parking lot to review the guidelines for David's second report. "Okay," Billy said, "just like your first report, you have two weeks to complete this report on *The Age of the Earth*. We've already visited Quantum Leap University as our first information source. So, the library will be a good second source from Ms. Lution's list."

"Yeah," David said. "Then it's Grand Canyon, here we come!"

"I can hardly wait," Darin said. Then he tipped back in his seat and pretended to be at the controls of an airplane. "If only Billy would let me pilot his plane, then this *Darin-bird* could really fly."

David laughed and turned to Billy. "You know, Ms. Lution was really excited to hear that I was going all the way to the Grand Canyon. She seemed relieved and told me, 'Now you'll be able to see the rock solid evidence with your own eyes—touch it with your own hands.' She went on to say that the Grand Canyon is one of the earth's greatest monuments to evolution—visible proof that the earth is millions, even billions, of years old."

Abel cocked one eyebrow up and scratched his head. "Uh, you know what I think? I think Ms. Lution is mixing up the evidence. I think she needs an expert on evidence to show her what the Grand Canyon really points to."

Darin looked at his brother in anticipation. "So, who do you suggest?"

Abel mussed his hair a bit, then grabbed Billy's trench coat out of the back of the jeep. "Lt. Columbo is on the job."

David hopped out of the jeep. "So, Lieutenant, it's like totally cool to get to meet you. Hey, I've got a question for you. I've always, like, wondered what your first name is."

"Shhh," Darin hopped out next to him. "That's a long-standing mystery."

"Not!" Billy scoffed. "I know what it is. Lt. Columbo's first name is Philip."

"Ha ha ha. *Wrong!"* the twins laughed. "I guess we know who's been playing Trivial Pursuit with Mrs. Carmen again. Obviously, you didn't know that *Philip* was just a made-up name put in by the maker of the original Super Trivia books."

"Then, what *is* his first name?" David pressed.

"Well," Darin shrugged, "really and truly, he doesn't have a first name at all. But the man who plays Lt. Columbo sometimes tells people his name is *Frank*."

At this point, the group entered the library. "Okay, gang," Billy said, "let's get to work." Billy and Abel went off to the computers, while David and Darin went to search the shelves.

"Hey, David-dude, look at this title, *Evolution, the Fast Creator*. If evolution is *fast*, then I guess God is greased lightning!"

David giggled and whispered, "And look at this one, *It Only Took 4.6 Billion Years*. Only? I guess some people don't consider that a long time.

"Oh, oh, look, here's one, *The Miracle of Evolution*. Somehow those two words just don't seem to go together," Darin said, rolling his eyes.

With that, David and Darin started a contest to see who could find the craziest book title. They were having so much fun that they forgot to stay quiet. So, pretty soon, a very cheerful-looking lady came down their aisle and whispered, "Please don't forget to use your *library voices*."

Darin and David both blushed and whispered, "Yes, m'am."

The librarian smiled at them both. "My name is Miss Informed. I'm a librarian here. Is there anything I can help you two find?"

"Excuse me," Darin questioned, in a confused voice. "Did you say that you're *misinformed*?"

"Yes," she answered with a pleased expression. "*Miss Informed.* I've always loved my last name—Informed. It's the perfect name for my job. Librarians are so *informed*, don't you think?"

"But, but," Darin sputtered, "you said that you were *misinformed*."

"That's right," she answered briskly, not catching on to Darin's confusion. "Now then, what is it that you're looking for?"

While Darin stifled a laugh, David spoke up. "We're looking for some good books explaining the evolutionists' view of the age of the earth."

"Oh, yes! You're in the right place." Then she asked, "Are you one of the honors students from Darwin School doing a report on how it took the earth billions of years to form?"

"Well," David said, "yes and no. I *am* doing a report for school. But actually, *my* report will refute the idea that the earth took billions of years to form."

"Goodness! I mean, that seems impossible. Just look around you. We have hundreds of books here, each filled with all kinds of things that basically *prove* that the earth is billions of years old."

Billy and Abel came up in time to hear Miss Informed's last statement. Abel responded in a perfect imitation of Lt. Columbo. "Ummm...what do you mean by *prove*, Miss? Are you sure you are not misinterpreting the evidence? I mean, what exactly *proves* that the earth is billions of years old?"

Miss Informed stared at Abel for a few seconds, then replied, "Well, let's see. Here, look at the ring on my finger. It's an opal. And we all know that opals take millions of years to form. So, if this opal is that old, of course the earth that it formed in is even older—much older."

Columbo answered, "Yes, Miss, I see how you could think that. But suppose—just suppose—there was a man in Australia who grew opals in his backyard laboratory, grew them, mind you, simply by mixing together the right chemicals—no heat, no pressure, *no* millions of years. Now, what would you say to that, Miss?"

"Those," Miss Informed shook her head, "would be synthetic opals. Any gemologist could see that they're fake."

"Ahhh..." Lt. Columbo continued, scratching his head. "I see. I see. But, what if these *synthetic*—or as you said, *fake*—opals where found to be indistinguishable from the opals mined in the opal fields? Indistinguishable," Abel added, "even under an electron microscope?"

Miss Informed looked to Billy for an explanation and asked, "Is he saying that there really is a man who really does produce *real* opals in his own backyard?"

Billy smiled his big smile. "Yes, m'am. Dr. Len Cram was awarded an honorary doctorate for his successful research."

"But, how is that possible? It's supposed to take millions of years to form opals."

Darin jumped in. "That's just it! We've all been taught that it takes millions of years. But really, that was just somebody's idea, and sometimes ideas turn out to be wrong. There's no real *proof* that it takes opals millions of years to form. But Dr. Cram has *proven* that it does *not* have to take millions of years to form an opal. With the right mixture of common chemicals, three months is all it takes."

Billy explained, "You see, the million-year opals are just a theory—man's idea. They aren't really operational science since they can't be..."

David finished, "...observable, testable, and repeatable."

"Right," Billy said. "Operational science must be observable, testable, and repeatable. You *can't* observe, test, and repeat opals mined out of the earth. But you *can* observe, test, and repeat Dr. Cram's three-month-old opals. They are a scientific fact."

David continued excitedly, "And just yesterday we had an interview with Dr. Hope Borton and Dr. Carl Osborne over at Quantum Leap University. They each showed us a piece of high-grade black coal. Dr. Osborne said that his piece of coal was mined from a coal bed that formed millions of years ago. Then he added, none too politely, that *real scientists* know how coal is formed, and that it's a *fact* that it's a slow and gradual process."

"But then," Darin jumped in again, "Dr. Borton showed us her piece of coal. She said that her high-grade coal was formed in exactly *13 weeks*. Man!" Darin laughed. "You should have seen the look on Dr. Osborne's face."

The librarian looked to Billy again. "Is what Dr. Borton said about *13 weeks* really true?"

Billy nodded. "Argonne National Laboratories have shown that by heating wood, acidic clay, and water to 150 degrees Celsius for between 4 and 36 weeks, high-grade black coal is formed. And, that was with no added pressure. Just the right ingredients under the right conditions."

"And," David said, "Dr. Borton let me hold it. I had proof in my hand—observable, testable, repeatable proof—that it does not have to take millions, or even thousands of years for coal to form. I was holding proof that, under the right conditions, coal can form in a matter of weeks."

The librarian looked upset. "But, this is ridiculous! I was taught in school that millions of years was a fact, and that opals and coal proved it."

Lt. Colombo shook his head with a sigh. "I'm afraid, m'am, that you've been...uh...*misinformed*." Everyone, including the librarian, had to laugh at Abel's joke.

"Well," she concluded, "I guess I *have* been *misinformed.* You've certainly given me something to think about. Perhaps we can talk about this more another time. But, for now, I'd better get back to my desk."

CHAPTER 6

A week later, David and the CSC were flying over Greenville in Billy's private plane.

"Super-colossal-great!" Darin exclaimed. "My bionic binoculars are working super-cali-fragil-istic! I can see everything down there." Then he shouted to Billy, "Hey! You're over David's house. Circle around it."

David looked out his window. "Where? Where?" Then he made a grab for the binoculars.

But Darin leaned out of his reach. "Look!" he said excitedly. "Your mom and sister are coming out. Hey! They're waving. They know…"

Suddenly, the plane banked sharply, and Darin screamed as he found himself hanging upside-down. He let go of his bionic binoculars and grabbed on to Abel. "Heee-yelp! Heee-yelp! What's happening?"

Only three seconds later, the plane was right-side up again—but now, the binoculars were in David's hands. "Thanks, Billy!" David said with a laugh as he focused the bionic binoculars on his mother's smiling (though a bit worried) face.

Darin was still holding tightly to Abel as he complained, "Hey! No fair, Billy! You know this *Darin-bird* doesn't like flying upside down."

****

To David, it seemed almost too soon when Billy told them they were approaching Grand Canyon National Park. But then, it seemed to take forever to land the plane, wait for a shuttle bus, and hike to the canyon itself. By the time they got there, everyone was tired and hungry. So, they decided to take a break for lunch before joining a tour group.

After a satisfying lunch, Billy tipped the bill of his cap over his eyes and leaned back against a sun-warmed rock with a sigh. "Ahhh…" he said, "I was made to be in the great outdoors."

David and the twins, however, were already rested and rarin' to go—up and exploring anything they could find. It only took Abel a few minutes to find what he was looking for—a group of flat rocks exposed to the full autumn sun. He stopped the others with a raised hand, then slowly and quietly approached the rocks. David and Darin joined him. Then Abel pointed to something on one of the rocks.

David and Darin had a silent tug of war over the binoculars. It looked like Darin was going to win, until David whispered, "You know, I've heard that Darin-birds don't like to fly upside down. I'm sure Billy would…"

Darin quickly let go of the binoculars, but whispered back, "Cheater! You're a cheater-bird!"

David just smiled and focused the binoculars on the object on the rock. "Oh! Awesome! It's a rattlesnake! And it's a big one. Let's get closer and try to measure it!"

But Lt. Colombo stepped forward. "I'm sorry, really sorry, but I'm afraid it's not safe in there. Only qualified personnel should enter such a dangerous area."

David was disappointed until he saw Billy creeping stealthily up on top of the rocks behind the snake. He had a long stick in one hand and a sack in the other. Then, with the skill that comes from lots of practice, Billy hooked the big rattler on the end of his stick and slid it into the open mouth of the sack.

Everyone waited impatiently for Billy to make his way cautiously out of the rocks. Then, they crowded around him. "Whoa!" he said. "Not too close."

He led them to a solitary flat rock about five feet high, and they all climbed up. Darin set his bionic binoculars to tele-pixal camcorder mode, while Billy lay down on his stomach and leaned over the edge of the rock to shake the snake out of the bag. As soon as it was free, it quickly coiled up and set itself to strike. Its tail rattled menacingly.

"Totally incredibly fan-creepy-tastic!" Darin whispered.

"Too cool!" David whispered back. "It looks like a Western Diamondback."

"Close," Abel said. "But the green tinge makes this a Mojave Rattlesnake. And it's a big one. I'd say over four feet and almost as thick around as my wrist."

After another minute, the snake settled down and slithered back toward the safety of the smaller rocks.

****

While the CSC was still sitting up on their rock, they were approached by a man in a tan uniform. "Hey," he said, "don't I know you guys?"

Darin shouted, "Look! It's the car-crash guy from Dr. Teddy's museum!" And so it was—Cliff Newman, the ticket taker. Everyone greeted each other in a friendly way. Then Cliff hopped up and joined them on the rock.

"So," Darin slapped him on the back, "I guess you're a park ranger just like you wanted to be."

"Not quite," Cliff laughed. "Right now I'm just a *ranger's assistant*. But I'm okay with that." Then he smiled self-consciously and told them, "I flunked the ranger's exam."

Everyone looked so serious and sorry that Cliff laughed again. "Don't worry, I flunked for a good reason."

"How can you flunk for a good reason?" David wondered.

"Like this," Cliff explained, "I took Billy's advice and started reading through the Bible. Then, I took my questions to a few creation science websites. The answers I found there made so much sense that I used that information to answer some of the questions on the ranger's exam, and…"

"And," Abel shook his head, "I'll bet those in charge coiled right up, ready to strike."

"Pretty close to it," Cliff admitted. "Anyway, they said that until they were sure I'd only answer visitors' questions with 'scientifically appropriate' answers, they couldn't put me in the position of a full-class ranger."

"It isn't always easy to stand up for the truth," Billy concluded. "But it's always worth it." Then, he suggested that Cliff join their group as their private tour guide. Everyone thought that was a great idea, and they set off to see what the canyon itself would tell them about its formation.

CHAPTER 7

By the end of the day, everyone was good and tired as they roasted some marshmallows before bed. Darin gave David a nudge. "Hey, dude, your marshmallow is burned to soot. Whatcha thinkin' about?"

David knocked the black marshmallow into the fire and started a new one. Then he tried to express what he'd been thinking about. "You know, we saw a lot of amazing and really beautiful stuff today. But, I can't help wondering what it's all gonna prove. I mean, evolutionists say it took millions of years to form the Grand Canyon. And, creationists say it was probably formed in a short time as the result of some catastrophic event."

David stopped to check his marshmallow, then continued, "I mean, I guess creationists really have the better argument, scientifically. But it all happened so long ago. No one really knows what happened except for God. And," he shook his head, "God doesn't exactly talk about the Grand Canyon in the Bible."

"You're right, David," Billy agreed. "The creationists have good theories, many of which they've proven are possible in laboratory experiments. But you can't quite hold the Grand Canyon in your hand the way you did Dr. Borton's lump of coal."

"Or one of Dr. Cram's opals," Abel added.

David sighed. "It just doesn't seem like what we've seen is going to make an impact on Ms. Lution. She considers the Grand Canyon, with its millions of thin rock layers, to be the evolutionists' *Holy Ground.* Isn't there anything that clearly upholds the creationists' view of short, catastrophic formation?"

Darin sneaked a glance at Billy. Billy winked, but shushed him with a quick shake of his head. Then he turned to David and encouraged him. "You know the expression, 'No one knows what tomorrow will bring.' But, for now, everyone to your tents for some well-deserved rest."

****

As the sun began to unveil the beauty of the early morning canyon, Billy was already helping David up a steep cliff. On a small landing, David looked up and across to the top of the opposite side of the canyon. Tiny versions of Darin and Abel were just visible. Mustering his courage, David let go of his climbing gear with one hand to wave in the direction of their binoculars.

It was only a minute before Billy was up beside him. "Here, David," Billy said, pointing to a place in the finely-layered rock wall. "This is just what we want. You hold the tape measure and I'll hold the info card." Billy held his card next to a specific section in the rock layers, then flashed a signal to Darin and Abel across the canyon.

"Hey, Abel!" Darin cried. "There's our signal. Now, I'll just trans-warp zoom in with my bionic binoculars...Okay, then to adjust for a steady focus...Now, I'll switch the setting to super-fab camera mode...Okay...There! I got five good close-up shots."

Abel met Darin in a leapin' high five. "Well, those were the last pictures we need." Then Abel continued in a secretive tone, even though they were a hundred yards away from anyone, "Do you think David suspects anything?"

"Naw!" Darin answered. "Billy's got the whole thing planned perfectly. So, we'd better hurry, or we'll get left behind." With that, they trotted off toward a waiting ranger's pickup.

Back on the small canyon ledge, David looked over the edge. "You know, Billy, I'm not so sure going down is going to be as fun as climbing up."

"Well, then," Billy remarked with a big grin, "let's go up instead." And he reached up and attached their climbing gear to a receiving rope that seemed to appear out of nowhere.

"Hey!" David exclaimed. "Where'd that come from?" But Billy's only answer was another big grin.

Nearly finished with his steep climb, David looked up to see the friendly hand of Cliff Newman reaching down to help him up over the top. "I should've known it was you. What's going on?"

But Billy quickly hauled himself up and said, "No time for questions. We've got a deadline to make. Let's get into Cliff's pickup and get movin'!"

Within the hour, they pulled into the small airport where Billy's plane was tied down. Abel and Darin were already there waiting. David hopped out of thc truck and begged Abel, "Come on, Abel-man, you'll tell me what's goin' on, won't you?"

Abel looked toward Billy and Darin, then cleared his throat. "Well, I don't see how it would hurt. Besides, as I'm Lt. Columbo, I *am* the boss." Still, he took another glance toward the others before he leaned over and whispered something into David's ear.

"What?" David shouted.

Abel tried to shush him and look innocent at the same time, but it was obvious that the cat was out of the bag. So, Billy wasn't very surprised when David came charging toward him asking, "Are we really flying to Mount St. Helens in Washington State?"

"That's right. You said you wanted something that would knock Ms. Lution's evolutionary socks off concerning the Grand Canyon. We're going to find just what you need at Mount St. Helens."

"Cool!" David said as he jumped into the plane. "Let's go!"

****

It was mid-afternoon before the CSC found themselves trekking toward the top of a large canyon carved out near the bottom of Mount St. Helens.

Looking down into the canyon before them, David shook his head in amazement. "Man! I can hardly believe I'm not looking at part of the Grand Canyon itself."

Billy nodded. "It was just formed in the eighties during the aftermath of the volcano's eruption—all in a matter of days!"

"Wow! Fan-catastrophic-awesome-tastic!" Darin had his *R.M.* glasses on and was viewing movie clips of the actual eruption of Mount St. Helens. David ran up behind him and snatched the glasses, then sat down and started viewing an assortment of *before* and *after* clips.

While David silently watched geological history being made, Darin and Abel unpacked and checked out the gang's climbing gear. Billy hiked ahead to scope out the canyon's edge for a suitable place to descend.

Once Billy had selected a good climbing location and the gear was all in order, David slipped off Darin's glasses and reached into his backpack to pull out a candy bar for everyone.

Chewing thoughtfully on his own candy bar, David turned to Billy. "You know, I'm not sure I really get it. I see the similarities in this canyon and the Grand Canyon, but what do those similarities prove?"

"Well," Billy began to explain, "it's making a connection between historical science, as in the Grand Canyon case, and operational science, as in this Mount St. Helens case. You see, with historical science, we can see the results, but we can't really know for certain the causes, just like with Dr. Osborne's coal. We can only make educated guesses based on the evidence. But with operational science, we see the results and we can *know for certain* the causes, like with Dr. Borton's coal.

"Now, because of the close similarities between this canyon and the Grand Canyon, we can make the reasonable conclusion that they were created by similar events. So, this observable event in front of us gives us great insight into the unobservable events of the past."

Darin jumped to his feet and, in an argumentative tone, insisted, "As a Grand Canyon official evolutionistic ranger, I tell you, 'a little bit of water and a long, long time carved the Canyon's incredible design.'"

"But," David responded, "*we know for certain* that this canyon in front of us was created by a whole lot of water in a very short time."

"Hmmm...well..." Ranger Darin fumbled for words. "Look!" he continued with a renewed confidence. "See all the Grand Canyon's thin rock layers—thousands and thousands and thousands of thin rock layers. Of course, they represent the hundreds of thousands of years it took to form the original rock bed the waters have carved through." Darin folded his arms across his chest as if he had won the debate.

Lt. Colombo scratched his head and sighed. "That's a mighty fine argument he's got there, Mr. David, sir. Is there anything you can say to defend your point of view?"

"Look right over there," David responded. "This Mount St. Helens canyon has lots and lots of thin layers, and we *know for certain* that all these layers were laid down in a very short time by the sorting of sediments in one big catastrophic event."

Columbo nodded, then went over to pat Darin sympathetically on the back. "Well, Mr. Ranger, in my job, the evidence rules. And, it looks like the evidence is ruling *against you* this time."

Billy laughed and gave David an approving smile. "Now you've got a good grasp on how observable science can give us some important clues into historical science." Then Billy shouldered his pack. "Well, we'd better get to work before we lose the light out of this canyon."

****

At the edge of one of the canyon's steep cliffs, Billy used Darin's binoculars and found just what he was hoping to see. "Look, over there is our ledge and the picture we want—the same fine-layered formation we photographed at the Grand Canyon."

Billy turned to Darin and Abel. "You two wait here while David and I hike over and up to that ledge to set up the tape measure and info card for another photo, just like we did this morning."

By five o'clock, David and Billy were back over with Darin and Abel. Abel had a micro-printer out and was printing off the pictures they had taken. Billy's eyes scanned the prints.

"There it is!" he cried. Abel quickly clipped that photo out and handed it to David.

David dug into his backpack and pulled out a carefully wrapped picture from the Grand Canyon. Then he jumped up and held the photos side by side.

"Look! Do you see? I have it! I'm holding it in my hand!" He held them higher and laughed. "I have eyewitness proof that, under the right conditions, a large canyon with a multitude of fine sediment layers doesn't have to take millions—or even thousands—of years to form. Look, right here," David shouted to mountain above him. "All these sediment layers were laid down in just a few hours. And this canyon was carved out in just one day!"

* * * * * * *

By nightfall, the CSC was back at camp. David was stretched out on his sleeping bag watching Darin and Abel scurry around—in and out of a few nearby bushes. Darin had his *R.M.* glasses on and kept calling, "Heee-yelp! Heee-yelp!" Abel was responding with cruel hissing sounds.

Billy put down his journal to watch the twins. "What are those two up to now?"

"As far as I can tell," David answered, "the rare *Darin-bird* is fluttering and flapping as fast as he can to escape Abel, the hungry 30-foot long Mojave rattlesnake."

"Well," Billy chuckled as he stretched out on his own bag, "those two sure know how to have fun."

CHAPTER 8

The Age of the Earth
(It Didn't Take a Million Years)

by David J. Avila

Introduction

The latest scientific ideas concerning the age of the earth show that there are *two* very different theories. One theory claims that the earth is several thousand years old, and the other claims that the earth is several billion years old. These conclusions are almost inconceivably different—like the difference between one single tree and a huge rain forest. However, both theories start by looking at the same observable facts (evidence), and then interpreting (making sense out of) this evidence in order to support their conclusions.

How is it possible that the same evidence can lead to such vastly different conclusions? It's because the billion-year scientists *and* the thousand-year scientists both interpret the evidence based on their own preconceived beliefs of how old the earth should be. A *true* scientist will look closely at both theories to see which one explains the evidence better.

Evolutionists begin with the assumption (belief) that evolution is true. For evolution to be true, the earth has to be billions of years old. So, evolutionists interpret the geologic evidence to show millions and billions of years.

Creationists begin with the assumption (belief) that the Bible is true. According to the history recorded in the Bible, the earth is about 6,000 years old. So, creationists interpret the geologic evidence to show thousands of years.

For this report, I will focus on some of the geologic processes evolutionists tell us take millions of years. I will show, using observable evidence, that these processes do not have to take millions of years. In fact, some of these geologic processes can happen in a matter of weeks, days, or even hours. In this way, I will show that the evidence confirms what the Bible says—it didn't take a million years.

Opal and Coal Formation

It is commonly taught that it takes millions of years to form opal, and therefore, the earth must be at least as old. Some opals are said to be 30, 60, or even 100 million years old. Obviously, this is not observable science. Evolutionists base this claim on their belief that geologic processes are almost always *very* slow and gradual.

However, there is an Australian researcher who grows opal in his own back yard (obviously in much less than a million years). All he does is mix together the right common chemicals—with *no* added heat or pressure. Even under an electron microscope, his opals look identical to those mined in the field—those said to be millions of years old. This is observable proof that opal does *not* need millions of years to form. In fact, it is observable, testable, repeatable proof that, with the right mixture of common chemicals, opal can form very quickly—in about three months.

The formation of coal is another geologic process that we have been taught takes hundreds of thousands, or even millions of years to complete. Again, this is evolution's assumption based on the belief that geologic processes are very slow and gradual. But, of course, no scientist has ever witnessed the process of coal being formed over hundreds of thousands or millions of years. So, it is *not* observable science.

However, scientists *have* witnessed the formation of coal in a matter of weeks (yes—weeks). The temperature used for this process was only 150°C, and there was no added pressure. When heating wood, water, and acidic clay in a sealed quartz tube, high-grade black coal has been formed in as little as four weeks. This observable science shows that coal does *not* require millions, thousands—or even one year—to form.

Fossil Forests

The *multiple levels of fossil forests* found in Yellowstone National Park have been used to convince people that the earth can't be only thousands of years old. Evolution interprets the evidence as follows: one forest grew up, was buried and petrified in place, and then a new forest grew up on top of that. Over time, as many as 50 forests grew up and petrified, one on top of the other. Evolutionists say this series of fossil forests would require hundreds of thousands of years to form, thus supporting their theory that the earth is very old.

But a closer look at the evidence tells a very different story. A look at the root systems of these fossil trees shows us what really happened. The trees were uprooted and carried away from where they grew, and then were deposited in this new location. A look at the cross-sections of trees from different levels show that they have the same ring patterns. This means that the trees at different levels in the petrified forest actually grew at the same time and were all originally part of the same forest. From the evidence, it seems *one* forest grew, was uprooted, moved to a new location, and then was buried in layers. This is not observable science, just a much better interpretation of the available evidence.

However, the eruption of Mount St. Helens in 1980 gives a clear (observable science) picture of this process. A forest near the volcano was uprooted and carried away to a lake by a giant volcanic mudflow. Most of the branches and long roots were torn off the trees, but the root balls were still mostly intact. These uprooted trees floated for a time, then sank in the upright position, and finally were buried by sinking sediment. These trees (trunks with broken roots) sank and were buried at different times and at different levels in the sediment, giving the appearance of several layers of upright forests. So, observable science shows that the multiple layers at Yellowstone National Park did *not* need hundreds of thousands of years to be put into place, but only the right conditions and a few short years.

Layers and Canyons

We have been taught that finely-layered rock formations prove a very old earth. Evolution assumes that fine layers were laid down at the rate of one or two per year. So, if you count the number of layers, you would have a good idea of the number of years involved. Based on this belief, evolution teaches that millions of layers, like those we see at the Grand Canyon, took millions of years to be laid down. This helps to support their belief that the earth is billions of years old. Though taught as fact, evolution's idea about the Grand Canyon's layers is only a belief, *not* observable science.

However, scientists *have* observed thousands of fine layers being laid down very quickly. In fact, laboratory experiments and larger natural occurrences have shown that all that is needed to rapidly produce many fine layers is particles of different sizes flowing in water or through the air.

The best example of this layering happened at Mount St. Helens in 1980. When this volcano erupted, it produced a 25-foot-thick deposit of thousands of thin layers—all in about three hours. So, it's clear that finely-layered formations do *not* require thousands or millions of years, only hours. However, this is not a belief, it is observable science.

A ranger at the Grand Canyon's edge would tell us that a little bit of water and a long, long time carved the canyon's incredible design. We are told that it took millions of years for the Colorado River to carve out the canyon. This is only a belief, taught to us as fact by evolution.

The fact is, a large surge of water can carve a canyon in a very short time. A town in Georgia once watched a 160-foot-deep canyon form in less than 150 years. It is now a state park, one of Georgia's seven natural wonders. Near Walla Walla, Washington, a 120-foot-deep canyon was formed in less than six days (not years—days).

Most impressively, at Mount St. Helens, a 100-foot-deep canyon formed in *one day*. It looks like a mini Grand Canyon (about 1/40th scale). It's clear that canyons do *not* need thousands or millions of years to form, but only a matter of days. This is not a belief, it's observable science.

Conclusion

The two main theories of the age of the earth begin with very different beliefs (assumptions) about how old the earth is. Each theory's idea of how long certain geologic processes take is based on this original assumption.

In order for evolution to be possible, the earth *must* be billions of years old. So, evolutionists interpret the geologic processes to indicate millions of years. And, because creationists believe the Bible, they interpret the geologic processes to indicate thousands of years. This results in the *huge* age difference between the two theories (compare 4,600,000,000 to 6,000). With such a *huge* difference, each theory needs to offer some solid scientific evidence to support their beliefs.

Although both theories begin with a belief, only one offers multiple examples of observable science to support their belief. Evolution *cannot* offer scientific, observable evidence that these geologic processes require millions of years. It would take a scientist millions of years to observe such a process.

Creation, however, *can* and *does* offer scientific, observable evidence showing that many of these geologic processes actually do happen in a matter of weeks, days, or even hours. Clearly, the evidence makes better sense when we begin with what the Bible says—it didn't take a million years.

* * * * * * *

After grading David's second report, Ms. Eva Lution sat staring at her classroom wall for a long time. A war of reason was raging in her mind. David's report did not *disprove* the evolutionary theory of a very old earth. In fact, it didn't even really *prove* the creationist theory of a young earth. However, David's report was full of solid scientific facts that shook up evolution's *need* for millions of years, while upholding the biblical account of the age of the earth.

Eva turned to her computer and began an e-mail to her father, Dr. Lution, Ph.D. times three:

TO: drevlution@science.qlu.net
FROM: evalution@science.qlu.net
RE: Honors Science Reports

Hi Dad.

My honors kids handed in their *Age of the Earth* reports yesterday. They were all pretty average—good research, but everything I've heard before—except for ONE.

David Avila wrote another spectacular report. The only problem being that he rejects evolution and believes what the Bible says—that the earth is relatively young.

I can hear you now: "How can you call a report *spectacular* if it totally rejects real science? The Bible is nothing but mythology!"

But, Dad—the Bible aside—David's report was loaded with irrefutable, observable proof that millions and billions of years just might not be the truly scientific answer.

-Eva

PART 3

The Origin of Species

CHAPTER 9

David Avila sat on a chilly bench inside a large enclosure. However, his mind wasn't sitting with him that cold afternoon. Instead, it was 600 miles out to sea off the coast of the small South American country of Ecuador. He was an explorer from the old days, discovering the mysterious creatures of the Galápagos Islands. There were gigantic land tortoises and *sneezing* sea lizards. There were also a wide variety of exotic sea birds, some with blue feet, others with red feet, and even some that blew their necks up into bright red balloons.

But David's mind was pulled back to his present reality as a streak of white came running into the enclosure. Billy was close behind. David jumped up and out of the way as Billy made a dive for the white tiger cub.

"Not even close!" David laughed.

Billy rolled over onto his back in the grass. "Man, those all-out dives hurt a lot more at 40 than they did at 30."

With a saucy little pounce, the cub landed on Billy's head, grabbed his cap, and pranced off.

But suddenly, out of nowhere, an orange cub landed squarely on its white sister and snatched the cap. Darin chased Orangey around David's bench three times before Whitey joined the chase and took her brother down. With the prize locked in her teeth, she headed up a large pile of rocks with Orangey right behind her. Together, they settled down to chew the cap to smithereens.

"Hey!" Darin called. "Come down here! That's Billy's favorite baseball cap!"

At that moment, Abel entered the enclosure. "It appears you gentlemen might need a little help," he said in a proper British accent. "Don't you know, chasing and yelling will do you no good with misbehaving cubs? You must talk to them with *authority*, telling them what you expect of them."

Abel turned to the cubs and growled and yowled up to them. Both cubs cocked their heads as if listening. Then, Orangey picked up Billy's hat and climbed down the rocks with Whitey behind him. Together they sat at Abel's feet. Billy reached out and took back his hat.

Darin and David stared at Abel, then at Billy in disbelief. "How did Abel do that?"

"Don't you guys know," Billy said as he put on his semi-shredded hat, "that Dr. Dolittle here can talk to the animals?"

****

The following Monday at school, Jack and Jill oohed and aahed at the pictures David had chosen to include in Ms. Lution's third report assignment of the year, *The Origin of Species*. The pictures were of David holding and playing with the white and orange tiger cubs.

"Man! David, that's so cool!" Jack said enthusiastically. "I wish the Creation Science Club was tutoring us!"

Jill laughed. "Yeah, at first, I thought Darin and Abel were kinda weird. But now I see that they're just a little *different*, and a whole lot more fun than Mrs. Jennings."

"But," Jack reminded her, "Mrs. Jennings does make good seven-layer cookies."

"But," Jill reminded him right back, "Mrs. Jennings doesn't take us to play with the baby tigers at the zoo."

David smiled. "It was lots of fun. I mean, I've been to the zoo a hundred times, but I never went looking for all the examples of variations within species. Giraffes, elephants, rhinos—all show variations within their species. Of course," he added with a grin, "it sure helped that Billy is good friends with the director of thc zoo."

"You're so lucky," Jill pouted. "Our tutor took us back to Quantum Leap University for *our* second information source. Talk about boorrriinngg!"

"Yeah," Jack sighed. "Our uncle, Dr. Osborne, just kept going on and on about what he called *the true miracle of life*. You know, how time and chance defied the odds and somehow formed a single living cell. Then, how time and chance defied the odds and somehow turned those single-celled organisms into a jellyfish. Then," Jack droned on in an imitation of Dr. Osborne's monotone, "time and chance, mutation and selection, time and chance, mutation and selection, blah, blah, blah, somehow developed all the variety of animal life we see today, including us."

"The more I hear about the theory of *mush to man*," Jill complained, "the less sense it makes. But," she added in a confused tone, "I guess it must be true since it's what everyone believes."

"Not really," David said. "That's just media-mania."

"What?" Jack and Jill questioned together.

David explained, "A recent poll showed that the majority of people in America actually rejects evolution, even though public education and the media have been cramming it down our throats all our lives."

"So the majority really doesn't believe in evolution?" Jill asked.

David went on, hearing the words of Abel Tadue come out of his own mouth, "The fact is, hundreds and hundreds of highly-educated scientists have rejected the theory of evolution as…impossible, preposterous, ridiculous—even crazy."

"Then how can Uncle Carl be so confident?" Jack asked. "I mean, ever since we started these reports for Ms. Lution, my dad's been trying to think things through from a biblical viewpoint. But, anytime he tries to discuss things from the biblical perspective, our uncle always argues him down."

"Uncle Carl always wins," Jill said in an angry tone. "It's not fair! Dad's the nicest guy in the world. I wish Dad could win, even just once."

"You know what I think?" David said with a gleam of inspiration in his eye. "I think you two need to join the Creation Science Club on our trip to my third information source—the Galápagos Islands."

CHAPTER 10

The sun glimmered off the midday ocean as the CSC, plus Jack and Jill, rowed their wooden boat toward one of the many rocky shorelines along Isabella Island—the largest of the Galápagos Islands.

"Here we are," Billy looked toward land, "the *birthplace of evolution*." Then, looking at the three middle school students, he explained, "In 1835, Charles Darwin made his famous voyage to these islands on the HMS Beagle. He used different animals from these islands as *proof* or evidence that evolution is a *fact*."

"Since then, however," Darin laughed, "a lot of what Darwin proposed about evolution has been shown to be just plain-old downright *wrong*."

"But," Billy continued, "even though many of his ideas and predictions turned out wrong, some scientists won't let go of their *big escape*—evolution. So, they honor Darwin as a great hero."

"What do you mean by their *big escape*?" Jill asked.

"Well, I think you've seen how some scientists use evolution to escape the existence of God," Billy explained as he continued rowing toward the shore. "Evolution is their *creator*. That way, they are accountable to no one. At least they like to think so."

All at once, Jack leaped to his feet. "Look! Marine iguanas!" he said, pointing excitedly. However, his sudden movements set the small boat rocking. Jack tried hard to regain his balance as the others worked to settle the boat. Everything seemed to be in slow motion until Jack decided to give up and just let himself fall over the side into the salty waters.

He came up to Jill's finger pointing right in his face. "Look!" she giggled, "a marine iguana!"

"Well, Jack," Billy laughed at his man overboard, "you're one step ahead of the rest of us. We'll all be in there soon enough."

Then Darin began passing out snorkeling equipment. "Now, remember you guys, I've attached a micro-camera between your eyes on the goggles. Whatever you're looking at, that's what the camera will be focused on. Just click the button on your wrist band to snap a digital photo."

As the gang put on their snorkeling gear, two huge white and black birds swooped down close, clacking their bills. Everyone ducked down…except for Abel. "Goodness, my dear fellows," he said in his British accent. "You all seem a bit nervous." Abel chuckled at his startled friends. "Well, I suppose I must claim some fault, as I did fail to inform you that I had asked my albatross friends—Albert and Annie—to patrol the waters for us. They were simply flying by to let us know that these waters appear to be shark-free."

Jack and Jill looked at David with a big question mark on each of their faces. David just shrugged his shoulders and said, "Don't you guys know that Dr. Dolittle can talk to the animals?" Then he lowered himself into the cool waters.

Soon everyone except Abel was in the water. Abel had agreed to take first shift staying with the boat—but only after Darin had promised him his dessert that evening.

Underwater was a whole new world. Everything—even the fish—swayed to the muffled pulses of the water. Billy, Jack, and Darin swam toward the rocky shore, while Jill and David stayed out near Abel and the rowboat.

Coming part-way out of the water, Darin whispered to Jack, "Look, dude! We're face-to-face with *the creature that ate San Juan*." The iguanas didn't seem at all alarmed by the three sets of goggle-covered eyes staring at them.

Billy backed away a bit and said with a smile, "They might not be as big as *the creature that ate San Juan*, but they do have a *secret weapon*."

"No way! They're harmless," Darin said as he started creeping forward. "Come on Jack, let's get some real fan-spectacular-tastic close-up shots."

Beneath the surface of the deeper waters, David pointed out to Jill something swimming close by. Neither one could figure out what it was. It was dark with a longish oval body and a long snakelike neck. It swam and darted about as quickly as a fish, but it had a sharp beak and webbed feet. Both kids moved in closer to get some pictures. Suddenly, another, and then another dark form broke into the silent underworld. In a rush, they all seemed to know right where to go. Each skillful hunter snatched a fish and then bobbed up to the surface, leaving only their paddling feet underwater.

David and Jill surfaced to watch the strange creatures. "Look, it's just some kind of duck," Jill said.

"No way!" David argued. "Look at their wings. They're way too small. And their beaks aren't rounded, they're pointed with a little hook on them. It must be some kind of penguin or something."

Back on shore, Jack and Darin had crawled in among a dozen or so iguanas basking in the sun. "Super-fantaz-awesome!" Darin whispered. "They hardly seem to notice us!"

Then, one of the biggest iguanas slowly turned to face Jack. He nodded his head a few times, and then, *"KERCHOO!"* Jack ducked his face toward the rocks. "Eeew! Gross, man. He just..."

Then, *"KERCHOO!"* Darin's hand went up to cover his own face. "Yuk!"

"KERCHOO! KERCHOO! KERCHOO!"

"Retreat! Retreat!" Darin shouted. "They're covering us with their slimy snot sneezes!"

"KERCHOO! KERCHOO!"

Billy, still a safe distance from the iguanas, threw back his head and laughed as Darin and Jack squirmed frantically back into the water. "I told you they had a *secret weapon.*"

****

The Creation Science Club explored the watery shoreline of Isabella until early evening. Then they headed back to the tourist ship anchored a ways out from the island.

On the ship, they were met by Dr. Hope Borton, the professor from Quantum Leap University. "Did you have fun?" she asked with a smile.

"Man, did we ever!" David exclaimed. Then they all started talking at once about everything they had seen.

"Whoa! Whoa!" Billy said. "First, let's all go wash up and change. Then we can talk about everything over dinner."

As eager as everyone was to talk, they were even more eager to eat, so dinner was a fairly silent affair. Then, Billy started the conversation. "Thank you, Dr. Borton, for getting us special permission to snorkel off-shore without a guide. The kids were great, and they didn't break any of the island rules."

Dr. Borton looked at David, Jack, and Jill. "I'm glad you all took the rules seriously. We have to do all we can to protect these islands."

Jack looked at Darin with a smirk and told Dr. Borton, "I think these islands can protect themselves. The shores are lined with snot-shooting machines."

"The marine iguanas were sneezing on them," Billy explained.

"It was an unprovoked attack," Darin complained. "They had no reason to slime us like they did."

Dr. Borton laughed. "Oh, Darin, they weren't attacking you. The iguanas spend so much time in the sea water, feeding on sea plants, that they take in a lot of salt water. Those sneezes are their special way of getting rid of the excess salt in their systems."

"Hey!" Jack said, "Saltwater crocs do that kind of thing, too, but they don't have to sneeze."

"But," David wondered, "Billy said that the iguanas that live farther inland don't do that. Is it just because they don't get so much salt in them?"

"No," Dr. Borton explained. "Those are land iguanas. Even if they did take in too much salt, their bodies wouldn't be able to excrete it in that manner. This ability has developed only in the marine iguanas."

"Wow!" Jack exclaimed. "So, it's like evolution says—There were these iguanas that lived on the land, then they started trying to find food in the water, and their bodies slowly gained all these cool changes to adapt them to their new environment."

"Yeah," Jill agreed. "David and I saw evolution, too. There were these duck things. Well, I guess they used to be ducks. But now, they're kind of like penguins. Maybe someday they'll be like the dolphins we saw swimming around our ship."

"So, that means evolution really *is* true," Jack said, looking kind of confused. "We saw it happening today with our own eyes."

Jill was disappointed. "And that means Uncle Carl *is* right with all his time and chance talk?"

"Hold on! Slow down." Billy held up his hands. "You guys are getting way ahead of yourselves. Before we go making hasty conclusions, let's look at the facts."

Dr. Borton stood up. "First, why don't we go back up on deck." Turning to Abel, she asked, "Did you and Darin figure out how to get my programs loaded into those *Reality Morphing* glasses?"

"You bet! Darin and I downloaded all the information you wired to us. I also linked them so that we'll all be seeing the same thing at the same time."

CHAPTER 11

Up on deck, the air was cool and inviting. The sun was low, but still reflecting brightly on the rippling waves. Several tourists talked excitedly about the sea lions playing around the boat. Dr. Borton and the CSC were seated looking out toward the water, but they couldn't see any sea lions. Instead, they were seeing beautifully filmed images of the Galápagos marine iguanas and flightless cormorants.

"A computer screen in your glasses. That is, like, so totally cool," Jack said enthusiastically.

"Okay, Jill," Abel said, "ask the glasses your question."

"Umm..." Jill hesitated. "I'm supposed to talk to my sunglasses?"

"Yeah," Darin assured her. "This program is interactive. Go ahead."

Feeling a bit self-conscious, Jill said, "Umm...sunglasses...is the flightless cormorant an...umm...intermediate example of one kind of animal evolving into another kind of animal?"

Everyone's glasses showed a close up of a dark-colored sea bird waddling awkwardly toward the water. It used its ridiculously short wings to maintain its balance. But then, once in the water, it became a graceful and efficient predator.

A computerized feminine voice spoke through the glasses. "Is the flightless cormorant an intermediate example of one kind of animal evolving into another kind of animal?" the voice reiterated. "Negative. The flightless cormorant is an example of an isolated group of cormorants adapting to their new environment. Mutations are changing some of their biological systems, and selection is choosing for those changed systems."

"What's that mean?" Jack asked.

The glasses showed a *normal* cormorant in flight. It landed on the water surface and then dove underwater. It *swam* through the water chasing a fish. The feminine voice responded, "Mutations are responsible for creating changes within an animal kind, but they *cannot* produce a *new* kind of animal."

Then David asked, "Why can't one kind of animal change into another kind through mutations?"

Before his eyes, clips of a scene from a popular animated movie appeared. First, it showed a single-celled amoeba swimming around, then changing into a double-celled amoeba, then into more and more complex forms, growing and changing until different forms of marine life filled the waters. Finally, one of the sea creatures made the leap onto land—the supposed great-granddaddy of all land-dwelling creatures.

The animation was beautiful and it all just seemed so feasible—a little change here, a little change there, and *boom*, you have a new kind of animal.

But the glasses interrupted the entertaining scenes. "Evolutionists claim that mutations and natural selection are the creators of increasingly complex life forms. Evolution takes us from single-celled organisms to fish, to frogs, to mammals, all the way to people. However, for a single-celled ameba to change into a fish requires the addition of multiple new structures and systems such as bones, muscles, scales, fins, gills, a heart, a brain, and so on. Evolutionists claim that mutations supplied all of these new, complex structures and systems that did not previously exist in the ameba."

The voice continued, "This is speculation—a belief—*not* operational science. Mutations have *never* been observed to cause the changes that could lead to the production of these new structures and systems, or to a new kind of animal."

Jack took his glasses off and looked at Dr. Borton. "So, if mutations can't produce new, complex structures and systems, or new kinds of animals, how do you explain all the variety of life around us?"

"Yeah!" Jill piped in. "Uncle Carl says that creationists believe that God made everything just how he wanted them and that they don't change. He says that's ridiculous, since science has proven that things *do* change and adapt."

Hope Borton answered, "That's a common misunderstanding about creation science. The reality is that most creation scientists *do* believe in change. We see it, too. And we marvel at God's wisdom to create his creatures with the genetic ability to adapt to their changing environments."

Billy explained, "Genesis chapter one tells us that God made everything—plants and fish and bugs and reptiles and mammals—all according to their kind. God created things according to their kinds, yet with an amazing ability to adapt and change within their created kinds."

Pointing toward the island before them, Billy continued, "Yes, I do believe that an isolated group of *normal* cormorants gradually changed into the *flightless* cormorants we see here. However, I do *not* believe that these birds are on their way to becoming some sort of fish-bird. They will always be birds. They are just adapting to their *new* environment through mutations and selection."

"Oh!" cried Jill, "I think I get it now. You're saying that God made things with more genetic information than we can see. And mutations act on that information to add to the variety."

"Right," Dr. Borton said. "And, God made it so that natural selection could sort through and bring out the useful genes to help living things adapt to their changing environments."

They all put their *R.M.* glasses back on, and two charts came up.

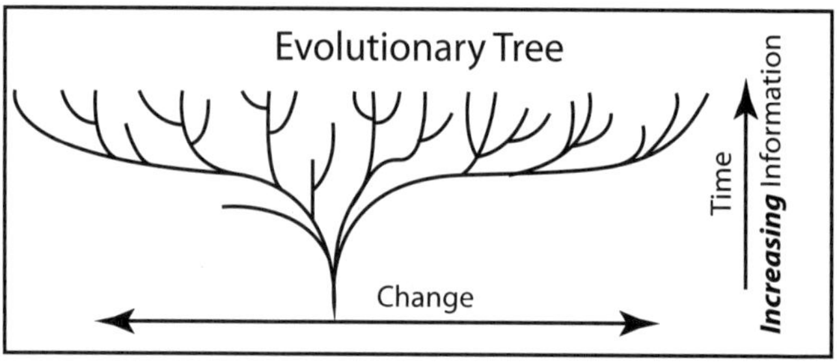

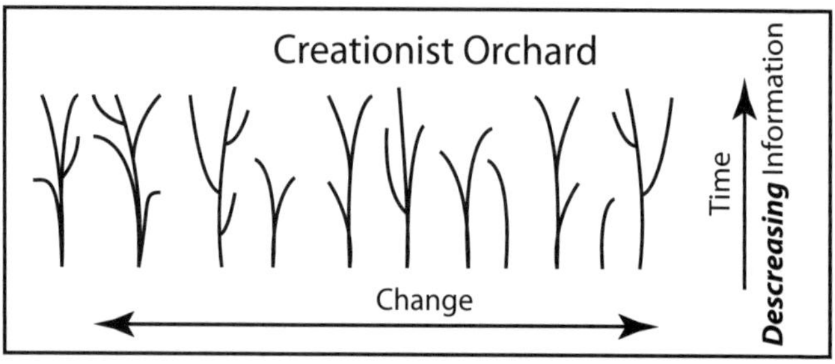

"I get it," David said. "According to the creationist *orchard*, the white and orange tiger cubs at the zoo are two branches off the *tiger* tree."

"Alert! Alert!" the glasses flashed. "Tigers are not considered a *tree* of their own in the creationist *orchard*." The glasses then showed many scenes of different cats—tigers,

lions, house cats, servals, bobcats, jaguars, even a re-creation of an extinct saber-toothed cat.

"Orange and white Bengal tigers are nearly identical genetically," the computerized voice explained. "They are simply two twigs on the Bengal tiger branch, which in turn belongs to the broader tiger branch which, in turn, belongs to the entire *cat kind* tree."

"Computer," Darin spoke to his glasses, "show us the *dog kind* orchard tree." Immediately an Australian dingo came to view, then a gray wolf, a fox, a large pet mastiff, and a tiny pet Chihuahua, and then, even a raccoon dog from Asia.

"Detail the wolf branch," Darin commanded. The glasses responded with a diagram of a branch off the orchard tree. Off the branch, new shoots grew out—a gray wolf, a red wolf, a Mexican wolf (or *Lobo*), and the now extinct dire wolf.

"More detail," Darin said. Detailing the gray wolf shoot off the wolf branch, the diagram showed small twigs growing out of it—an all gray wolf, an all black wolf, a mostly white wolf, a smaller-sized wolf, and a very large wolf.

"Wow!" David said. "God sure provided for an amazing amount of variety and potential to change when he created the cat and dog kinds."

"Yes," Dr. Borton said. "But the key is that they are still *dogs* and *cats*, they have not changed into new kinds of animals."

"People are the same way," Billy said seriously. "Some are big, some small; some light, some dark; some strong, some weak; some artists, some mathematicians. But we're all still people." Then he stood up with a stretch and said, "Come on, guys, we'd better head off to bed. Tomorrow will be a busy day at Darwin Station over on Santa Cruz Island."

****

Several days later, back in Greenville, David sat by the wood-burning stove in the CSC cabin on Maple Hill. He smiled as he told the gang about Jack and Jill's conversation with their uncle, Dr. Osborne.

"Even after they told him all they had seen and learned at Galápagos, he still talked to them like they were babies. He said, 'Those are some interesting ideas. But you kids are forgetting that we are talking about millions and billions of years. Little changes over a long, long time become big changes. Who knows what all can happen over the course of millions of years?'

"Then Jill jumped right in, 'That's right, Uncle Carl, who knows? Do you know? Actually, no one really knows. It's all speculation, just a belief. But,' she went on, 'what we *do* know is that observable science has never seen a mutation leading to a new, complex structure being produced that never existed before.'

"Then Jack tried to explain," David continued. "'Look, Uncle Carl, the theory of evolution relies completely on the fact that mutations, over time, can produce bones and muscles and scales and brains. But, even *millions* of years can't produce a new kind of animal if we can't observe mutations producing those new, complex structures and systems today.'"

"Well," Billy said, "it sounds like they won that debate."

"Yep!" David said with satisfaction. "Jack and Jill said that their dad can't wait to read their next report. He's so excited to finally get some evidence to back up what he's really believed all along."

Meanwhile, in the corner, Abel and Darin were arguing over one of the pictures Darin had taken at Darwin Station. It was a photo of a large land tortoise.

"You're wrong," Darin said emphatically. "I remember. This is Lonesome George, the last tortoise of his subspecies."

"No, sir, you are in error," Abel answered in proper British. "His name is Christopher. His mother named him after Christopher Columbus."

"Now, how on earth would you know that?" Darin said in an exasperated tone.

Billy gave David a wink and said, "Come on, Darin, don't you know by now that Dr. Dolittle can talk to the animals?"

CHAPTER 12

The Origin of Species
(Created After Their Kind)

by David J. Avila

Introduction

The latest scientific ideas concerning the origin of species show that there are *two* very different theories. While both theories look at the same observable facts, they come to very different conclusions. This is because both theories begin with a *different belief* about the origin of species. Then they try to interpret (make sense out of) the *same evidence* based on their different beliefs. A *true* scientist will look closely at both theories to see which one explains the evidence better.

Evolution begins with the assumption that all the species we see today evolved from a single-celled organism. They claim that the *small* changes we observe today (mutations and natural selection) have produced the *big* changes (evolution) over millions of years. Evolutionists begin with this belief and then try to explain the evidence.

Creation begins with the assumption that the Bible is true. According to the Bible, God created all living things after their kind. Creation claims that the *small* changes we observe today (mutations and natural selection) have produced an amazing amount of variation and adaptability within the created kinds. Creationists begin with this belief and then try to explain the evidence.

For this report, I will focus on the origin of species based on genetic change. I will show that mutations and natural selection are not producing the new, complex systems and organisms necessary for evolution to be true. Instead, we observe mutations and selection producing amazing variety and adaptability within the created kinds. In this way, I will show that the evidence makes better sense when we begin with what the Bible says, that all things were—created after their kind.

Genetic Information

DNA is a set of instructions stored in living cells. There is an incredibly huge amount of genetic information stored in a single cell. One evolution scientist said that there is enough information capacity in a single human cell to store all 30 volumes of the Encyclopedia Britannica, three or four times over. One creation scientist said that a pinhead's volume of DNA can store the same amount of information as a pile of paperback books 500 times as tall as the distance from the earth to the moon.

So, we see that both evolutionists and creationists recognize the huge amount of information stored in DNA. And both agree that there is change in that genetic information through mutation and selection. But, evolution claims that we "see evolution all around us." For this to be true, we would need to see mutations leading to new, complex systems and organisms. Creation claims that we *do* see change, but we do not see mutations leading to new, complex structures and systems. Instead, we find amazing variation and adaptability within the created kinds. So, let's see how the two different theories explain the change we see in genetic information today.

The *evolutionary tree model* shows that all the species we see today have descended from a common ancestor. Evolution says that nonliving matter spontaneously became a living cell, which evolved into a jellyfish, then into a fish, a frog, and on down the line (or up the tree).

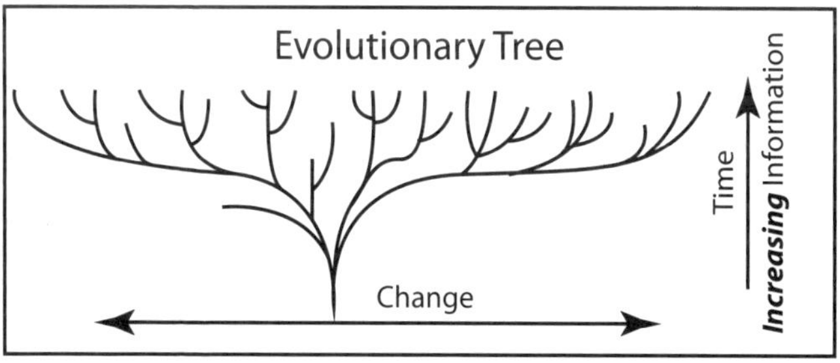

For this model to be true, there needs to be a massive *increase* in complex genetic information producing new systems and organisms. There must be *new information* that can form eyes, bones, hearts, scales, fins, legs, lungs, and so on. In the evolutionary tree model, the first simple cell did not have this information, so it had to be added. Evolution claims that mutations and natural selection have produced the new information and systems leading to the variety of life we see today.

The *creationist orchard model* shows that all the species we see today have descended from their created kinds. Creationists believe there was an incredible amount of variety and potential for change in the original genetic information in each created kind. For example, we can see from the amazing variety of dog breeds today that the original dog kind held an incredible amount of variety in its genetic make-up. Creationists believe that mutations and selection acted on this information to enable their descendants to adapt to different environments and needs.

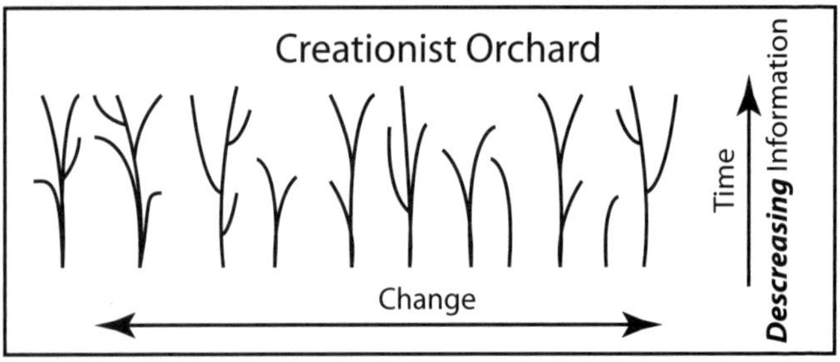

For this model to be true, we should see mutation and selection producing variety and adaptation within the created kinds. In the creationist orchard model, we shouldn't see new, complex information and systems leading to new *kinds* of creatures.

Mutations and Natural Selection

Both theories on the origin of species observe changes going on among living organisms. And, both sides agree that mutations and natural selection are causing the changes we see. But, evolution claims that these processes are producing the new, complex genetic information and systems necessary for evolution to be true. Creation, on the other hand, claims that information is being *sorted and changed*, but *no new, complex systems* are being produced. Here, at the genetic information level, the two theories disagree. *So*, which one makes better sense of the evidence?

Mutations are changes within the genetic make-up of a *single* organism. When a cell reproduces, a copy of its DNA is made. Sometimes there is a copying error, called a mutation. Usually, mutations are harmful. Consider a species of long-legged lizards. A lizard born with short, stubby legs would not be able to outrun its number one enemy—the coyote.

However, occasionally, a mutation turns out to be helpful. This would be true if that short-legged lizard turned out to be much better at climbing trees, enabling it to more easily escape coyotes. Some would claim the short-legged lizard's survival to be the result of evolution—one step toward gaining new, complex systems. But that's just not true. Mutations are errors. A series of spelling mistakes will never produce a novel. A million years of mathematical mistakes will never lead to a computer program. And mutations, whether harmful or helpful, have *never* been observed to produce the kinds of complex genetic systems found in the variety of life we see today—no evolution.

Natural selection is a change in the genetic information found *within a group* of organisms. Natural selection 'chooses' the genetic qualities from within the group that are *best fit* for the group's survival. If some lizards in a group are born with long legs, and others are born with short, stubby legs, natural selection would select the lizards *more fit* to survive and have offspring.

Now, since coyotes can't climb trees, the short-legged lizards would be *more fit* because they can more easily escape. So, the short-legged lizards would be more likely to survive and have offspring. The next generation would have more short-legged lizards. Over time, natural selection could produce a group of mostly short-legged lizards. Some would claim this change in the group to be the result of evolution, but that's just not true. Natural selection can only sort from *existing information*, it *cannot* produce new, complex systems and new organisms—no evolution.

Examples from Galápagos

The Galápagos Islands hold a unique variety of animals for the study of the origin of species. When certain types of animals first came to the islands, the following generations showed how mutations and natural selection led to changes in genetic information. But, are these observed changes better explained by evolution or creation?

The *flightless cormorant*, according to evolution, is awkward and imperfect. It looks like it's wearing a set of clothes that don't fit right. They say it's half way down the evolutionary track—in the middle of change from one kind of animal to another. But actually, this doesn't explain the evidence. We *do* see mutations and natural selection changing the genetic information of these birds. But we *don't* see the new, complex systems that would be necessary if evolution were truly happening—if these birds were truly changing into a different kind of animal. We only see existing systems changing and adapting.

The *marine iguana*, found only in Galápagos, is the world's only known sea-feeding lizard. According to evolution, it wasn't created or designed this way. It evolved (gained new, complex systems) to adapt to life on the islands. According to creation, the iguana *was* created and designed with enough genetic information to be able to adapt to a variety of environments. Creation explains the evidence—mutations, sorted by natural selection, produced an animal (after its kind) adapted to its new environment. We *do* see the change, but we *don't* see even one tiny step toward the increase in complex systems necessary for evolution to be true. Their change was the result of existing systems adapting to a new environment.

Finally, "Darwin's" finches, according to evolutionists, are by definition an example of evolution. But if we look at the genetic information, this statement is simply not true.

Finches have enough genetic information to change (adapt) to various conditions and food sources. A variety of beaks can be produced by mutations and natural selection. No new systems are needed (or observed)—no evolution.

Conclusion

Any scientific theory concerning the origin of species must explain the incredible amount of genetic information and change we observe in living organisms today. According to evolution, all the species we see today evolved from an original single-celled organism. They claim that mutations and natural selection, over hundreds of millions of years, have produced the complex systems and variety of life we observe today.

According to the Bible, God created all living things after their kind—God created the genetic information in the beginning. Creation claims that a sorting and change of the created genetic information has produced the amazing variation within the created kinds we see today.

It is true that we see changes in living organisms all around us. But the claim that "we see evolution all around us" is false. Mutations and natural selection are not producing the new, complex systems and organisms necessary for evolution to be true. Instead, we observe mutations and selection producing amazing variety and adaptability within the created kinds. To any objective scientist considering both theories, clearly the evidence makes better sense when we begin with what the Bible says, that all things were—created after their kind.

****

Leaning on the wall surrounding the Hansen Zoo's tiger exhibit, Ms. Eva Lution watched the white and orange tiger twins chase each other around their resting mama. In her mind, she herself was a young child begging her own mother, "Again! Sing it again!" And her mother would laugh and take hold of her hands to dance once more through their favorite song:

> "A is for Antelope, B is for Butterfly,
> C is for Cheetahs that go running by.
> God made each and every thing.
> God is the Maker of everything.
>
> "D is for Dinosaur, E is for Eagle,
> F is for Foxes that go running by.
> God made each and every thing.
> God is the Maker of everything…"

Ms. Lution laughed as the mama tiger skillfully pinned Orangey under one paw and began washing his face with her rough tongue. In her thoughts, Eva saw herself snuggled in bed after a bath with her own mother smiling down at her. "Well, Evangeline, my little queen, what shall I read from your Bible tonight?"

Evangeline Lution didn't have many early memories of her father. He had always been busy reading, researching, writing, and teaching. Even then, she had known that her dad was considered "a genius." And she was proud of him. But she had felt sad that he wouldn't go to church with her and Mom. "You go sing with your mother, Eva," he would always say. "I need to stay home and try to figure out the universe."

After washing up her cubs, the mama tiger led them into the warm and private section of their enclosure. But Ms. Lution didn't even notice they had left. Once again, she was a child. Her mother had died. Her dad was very sad. Wanting to cheer him up, she had run up to him, taken hold of his hands, and pulled him around and laughed. "Let's sing, *God Made Every Thing*!" But her father had nearly shouted at her. "No, Eva! I don't want you to sing that anymore." Then he had continued sternly, "Your mother is gone now. No more fairy tales. From now on, you are going to learn about science."

From that time on, Eva had accepted that science was godless. *But now, for the first time*, she was seeing real science with real answers that did not discredit God. Instead, the science she was reading about in David Avila's reports definitely pointed to a Creator God. If God was the Creator of the heavens and the earth, then He was also the Creator of Evangeline Joy Lution.

As this realization settled into Ms. Lution's heart, a great weight seemed to lift from her shoulders. Suddenly, she felt free. For the first time since her mother's death, she actually felt like singing.

PART 4

The Complexity of Life

CHAPTER 13

High up on Maple Hill, a voice called out through the chilly autumn air, "David! Abel! Where are you guys?" Darin Tadue tramped along through the fallen leaves, grumbling to himself. Then he stopped and yelled again, "Come on, you guys! I want my bionic binoculars back." When he again received no answer, Darin pulled a pair of *R.M.* glasses out of his jacket pocket and spent a minute setting them to a *heat-tracking* mode. "Boy, will they be sorry they decided to try and hide from *me*," he said with a self-satisfied smile.

Only a minute later, Darin found the trail he was looking for. Footprints showed up warm red through his glasses. Following the trail with his eyes, Darin could see a patch of bushes on ahead that were glowing red. Slowly, silently he reached into his hip pocket and pulled out a slingshot. Then, reaching into his shirt pocket, he pulled out a large, soft pellet. On the pellet were printed the words *Super Stink-Bomb Ammo*.

Darin's smile was getting bigger and bigger as he pulled his noxious ammo farther and farther back in the sling shot. Then, he took a final step forward, ready to let it fly…

"Whoa! What! Heee-yelp!" Darin flapped helplessly around in circles as he found himself hanging upside-down by his ankles.

"You caught him!" David jumped out from behind the bush and laughed at the sight of his upside down friend.

"Well, now, Boy!" A deep-woodsy kind of a voice responded. "Didn't I tell you that Davy Crockett was the best trapper that ever thar was?" The voice, of course, belonged to Abel.

As Darin continued flapping in circles, Abel scratched his head and added in his normal voice, "I wonder if Davy Crockett ever caught a Darin-bird?"

Later that day, the Creation Science Club sat around a cozy fire eating popcorn at their log cabin headquarters.

"Do you see?" David said excitedly. "Ms. Lution changed the fourth report topic from *The Evolution of Your Favorite Animal*, to *The Complexity of Life*. See! She completely cut out the word *evolution*."

"Whoa! David-dude," Darin exclaimed. "Could Ms. Eva Lution, the *Queen of Evolution*, be ready to take off her crown?"

"Well," Billy put in, "you know, her real name is Evangeline. There's always hope with a name like that. But, for now, we'd better start planning this report." Then, turning to David, he asked, "So, what animal have you chosen?"

David looked a bit discouraged. "I don't know. I like all kinds of animals. But, I want to pick something *special*."

"How about…" Billy started to say.

"The *bald eagle!"* Darin interrupted. "Majesty in motion."

"No," Billy cut back in. "The *grizzly bear!* Power, courage, and beauty all in one."

"The grizzly?" Darin snorted. "It's nothing but a fat hair ball with bad breath."

"Excuse me!" Abel stood up. "I have the *perfect* favorite animal."

"What is it?" everyone asked, turning toward him.

"The *Schnoodle!"*

The others looked at him blankly. "What's a…schnoodle?" David finally asked.

"It's this cute little designer dog I read about yesterday—part miniature schnauzer, part toy poodle."

"The bald eagle would eat your schnoodle for breakfast!" Darin shouted. "I'm telling you, pick the eagle."

Billy raised his own voice. "My grizzly could eat that schnoodle-dog *and* your eagle for a mid-morning snack!"

"A pom-poo, then!" Abel joined in the shouting.

David shook his head. "Abel, I don't think Davy Crockett would have approved of a pom-poo."

"Eagle, eagle, eagle," Darin chanted as he spread out his arms and "soared" around David. "Majesty in motion."

Billy stood up and flexed his impressive biceps. "The grizzly—raw power!"

"How about a peek-a-poo, or a puggle?"

David fell back on the couch and covered his ears. "Guys, I can't choose based on who shouts the loudest. I think you're just gonna have to prove which is the best."

"Okay," Billy said. "I *will* prove it! With your parents' permission, we're going to take a trip to Yellowstone National Park. There you can see and choose for yourself."

Davy Crockett shook his head and sighed. "I'm havin' some serious doubts about seein' any cute lil' dee-ziner dogs over thar."

****

Later that week, David sat at a study hall table with his friends, Jack and Jill. It was the last period of the day, and they were all just kind of staring out the window. Suddenly, David jumped up. "Hey, look out on that tree!"

Hopping up and around on the tree's trunk was a fairly large, dark-backed, light-breasted bird. On the back of its head was a large red spot. The bird stopped and began to peck at the bark.

"That's a Red-bellied Woodpecker," Jack told him. "They're pretty common," he added in a bored tone.

But David was fascinated. He watched until the bird flew away. Then he said to himself, "Fan-taz-cool-o-rama!"

Just then, Ms. Eva Lution entered the study hall room. David quickly returned to his seat, and all the students immediately looked intently at their schoolbooks. No one said a word. Every kid in the room had felt the whip of her tongue at some point during their time at Darwin Middle School.

Ms. Lution looked around the room, then walked up to David's table. Looking at Jack and Jill, she said, "If you twins would please excuse us, I would like to discuss David's past science reports with him...*alone*."

Jack and Jill jumped up and quickly moved to another table. The whole room held its breath. Everyone felt sorry for David. They knew he had been pretty outspoken about his Christian beliefs. They knew that, up to this point, Ms. Lution had totally rejected any theory other than evolution. It looked like David's time had finally come. Would he get kicked out of the honors science class? Would he be suspended? Or even expelled?

But, after a brief conversation, Ms. Lution calmly stood up, smiled at David, and left the room. The whole study hall, including the monitor, finally began to breath again. David didn't look at all upset. Instead, he looked excited. Jack and Jill hurried back over to his table.

"Man, dude!" Jack said. "We all thought you were a goner for sure!"

Jill couldn't contain her curiosity. "What did she say? You have to tell us!"

"Well...she said that she's been thinking about how she grew up seeing only one side of the *origin of life* debate—the evolution side. She thought maybe she should try looking at things from a new perspective. So," he added with a nervous little laugh, "she asked if she could join the Creation Science Club on our trip to Yellowstone National Park this weekend."

Jack and Jill's mouths dropped open.

"Scary, Man!" Jack whispered.

"You can count us *out* on this one," Jill said, shaking her head.

CHAPTER 14

High up in the forest-covered hills, a bull elk turned its immense antlers toward the new sound. Its large eyes easily spotted the distant group of visitors, and its sharp ears could make out every word of the song they were singing as they worked their way up a steep hill. "We're marching to Zion, beautiful, beautiful Zion. We're marching upward to Zion, the beautiful city of God..."

Pawing at the cold ground, the elk turned and disappeared into the woods. Many other forest animals also ran from the hikers. In fact, alerting the animals of their approach was the main reason the group was singing. For this was grizzly country, and everyone knows grizzlies *hate* surprises.

As thc trail leveled out, the gang stopped singing to catch their breaths. Ms. Lution shook her head and laughed. "Goodness, Mr. James, you sure know a lot of songs!"

Billy smiled. "Singin' is one of the loves of my life—not that I do it all that well. But I sure do enjoy it."

Ms. Lution looked thoughtfully at the October forest around her. "I remember my mother once saying that very same thing."

"Look!" Abel exclaimed, pointing toward a medium-sized darkish bird with a red crown and a red chin. "It's a Red-napped Sapsucker!"

Immediately, David and Darin began their *now familiar* tussle over Darin's bionic binoculars. When David saw that he wasn't going to win this time, he quickly focused his own *regular* binoculars on the bird. As the bird hopped around looking for hidden bugs, David just stood still and watched. "So way cool!"

"Yeah…" Darin agreed. "But just wait till you see a *bald eagle*." Then he added, "I'm betting you'll choose the eagle for your report."

"Nah!" Billy huffed. "Ten to one he'll pick the *grizzly*. There's nothing so awesome as an autumn grizzly!"

While Darin and Billy bantered back and forth, Ms. Lution fell in step with Abel. "So, I hear you're working on your Masters degree in Zoological Biometrics. That's pretty impressive for a 17-year-old."

Abel shrugged modestly. "Not so impressive as you might think. Darin and I *cheat*, ya know."

Ms. Eva stopped in her tracks. It seemed preposterous that these nice boys would really cheat. "What do you mean *cheat*?" she asked.

Abel laughed at her expression of disapproval. "Well, I guess it isn't our fault we're cheaters. So, I guess technically it really isn't *cheating*."

"Okay," Ms. Eva said, with one eyebrow raised, "explain yourself, young man!"

Abel shrugged again. "It's just the way we were born. With Asperger Syndrome, it's genetically natural for us to hyper-concentrate on very detailed issues. When we dive into a topic, we never get bored. We just soak it all in like a sponge."

"Wow, I guess that could be a real gift." Ms. Eva looked thoughtful. "I'd have to admit that I was pretty bored with about 75% of my scholastic studies. I guess that's why I never completed my dissertation. I mean, good grief, how can anyone write 400 pages about how advances in evolutionary recombinant genetics are positively affecting microbiological technology? I think I would have rather studied literature—there's so much more *life* in that."

Abel's eyebrows drew down. "I love to read, but *not* literature. Give me a science book or a computer manual any day—the more technical, the better. They make sense to me. But *literature*...nope. I just can't even begin to understand the emotions and feelings the author is trying to express through the characters. It's like crusty old bread to me."

Eva smiled. "So, I guess I can admire you and Darin, but I really can't envy you."

Abel thought for a moment, then replied, "That's just how we feel about you non-Asperger folks. We admire what you have, but we don't envy you. Just like we can never really understand what you 'normal' people have, you can never really understand the intricacies that we Aspie folks enjoy.

"To be honest, Darin and I have had some hard times when people didn't understand the way we are or made fun of us. But, since we have so many good friends that accept us just the way we are, we wouldn't want to be anything else. We might see colors differently than you all, but they are just as bright—and, sometimes even brighter."

****

The group had traveled another couple of miles and was now well off the trail, heading toward an opening in the trees about 50 yards ahead.

Suddenly, from somewhere behind them came a low coughing sound, followed by a deep growl. Darin and David swung around with their walking sticks raised. Ms. Lution tried to stifle a scream. But Billy just laughed. "Come on, Abel, you can *smell* a grizzly before it gets that close!"

Then David and Darin laughed, too.

"That was pretty good, Bro," Darin said. "Better than your cougar one."

Ms. Lution tried to laugh, but just felt more nervous than ever. She was not really the outdoor type.

"Ain't no reason to be worried at all, Miss," that deep *woodsy* voice assured her. "Billy, here, be the best woodsman around—next to myself, of course."

Ms. Lution relaxed a little. "And who, sir, are you?"

"Why, Davy Crockett, of course," Abel replied. "King of the wild frontier."

"Oh, give me a break," Darin moaned. But everyone laughed, and Ms. Lution found herself feeling more and more a part of this strange little group of adventurers.

Coming out into the open, the sun felt warm on their faces. A careful climb down a slope led them to a large, rocky ledge. A few bare shrubs and several small evergreens made the ledge a kind of hide-away—like a natural *blind* for observing wildlife without disturbing it.

Billy explained, "Actually, Carmen and I found this ledge two years back while we were filming for a creation science conference out west." He looked around with a smile. "We ended up camping right here for the entire two weeks. Just check out the view!"

David walked forward. Looking out, he was amazed. Silently he sat down, lost for words. Out over the rocky ledge, the world dropped down about 100 feet to a large, twisting stream. Even as he looked on, a small group of elk approached the water for a drink.

Everyone sat quietly, content to watch the elk. But then, one elk raised its head. Nervously, the others looked around. They stamped the ground, then turned and bounded back into the trees. Billy pointed up stream. Barely visible, something big and brown was moving toward an opening in the trees. It was a bear—a grizzly.

Everyone put their binoculars to their eyes. But Darin, with his bionic binoculars, drew their attention to something still back in the trees. Two smaller brown shapes—cubs!

Mama Bear came out to the stream's edge. Shaking her head back and forth, she coughed and huffed. Then, rising on her back feet to her full impressive height, she seemed to be sniffing the air.

Billy explained, "She can smell us. Bears have an incredible sense of smell."

Davy Crockett added, "She won't be calling them cubs out of the woods till she's sure it's safe."

When Mama Bear finally decided things were okay, she turned to the woods and called her cubs. The cubs were not the small, weak cubs of spring. They were medium-sized, well-fed, and rambunctious. They shot straight past their mama and right into the stream.

"So, David," Billy asked, "isn't the grizzly a creature worthy of your report?"

But before David could answer, Darin jumped up. "No way, dude! Look over there!"

They all saw a large, dark bird swooping close over the stream. Suddenly, it dipped, letting its feet hit the water. Then it veered up, carrying a struggling fish in its talons. "Incredible!" David almost shouted. "A bald eagle! And it just caught a fish!"

"So, David," Darin asked, trying to mimic Billy's voice, "isn't the eagle a creature worthy of your report?"

David could only answer, "They're both awesome. Surely God is *the* Master Designer!"

Ms. Lution smiled at David's enthusiasm, but then her face clouded with doubt. She turned to Billy and said, "Part of me wants to have the *simple faith* that David has. But," she searched for the right words, "faith is…just faith, while evolution is based on scientific facts."

Billy shook his head. "Ms. Lution, you're mistaken. You've heard 'evolution is based on facts' over and over until you just believe it. I mean, what do all these great intellectual scientists really *know* next to God?"

Ms. Lution thought about what he said, but then looked back down at the bears without responding.

"See those bears?" Billy continued. "It takes a lot more *blind faith* to believe that the perfectly-equipped grizzly—or elk, or eagle—just somehow evolved through millions of years of genetic mistakes. Evolution isn't even scientifically sound. Only a fool…"

"Mr. James!" Ms. Lution interrupted sharply. "My father is no fool. He is a genius. And he has studied and believed in the theory of evolution most of his life."

"Ms. Lution," Billy said more gently, "many intelligent scientists have spent entire lifetimes and billions of dollars trying to find one solid fact that would *prove* evolution. But, so far, no such fact exists. There are theories, ideas, misconceptions, and outright fraud, but no facts.

"On the other hand," Billy continued, "there are countless scientifically sound examples that point to a *Master Designer*. Evolution is direct rebellion against God. Romans chapter one explains it like this—people 'suppress the truth by their wickedness, since what may be known about God is plain to them, because God has made it plain to them.'"

David felt uncomfortable seeing his mentor and teacher in such an intense debate. He turned to Abel and said, "Hey,

Davy Crockett, why don't you use your woods-sense to lead us to whatever's making that pounding sound."

"Yeah!" Darin joined in. "Maybe someone is building a secret hide-out or something. Let's sneak up on him!"

"I'll bet," David guessed, as they climbed up the steep hill, "it's a bank robber building a box to bury his stash in! If we catch him, we'll get a huge reward..."

So, while Abel led David and Darin off to investigate the mysterious sound, Billy and Ms. Lution continued their conversation.

"What do you mean," Ms. Lution asked in frustration, "by *made plain*?"

Billy explained, "Romans one continues, 'Since the creation of the world God's invisible qualities—his eternal power and divine nature—have been clearly seen, being *understood* from what has been made...' that is, through *creation*...'so that men are without excuse. For although they knew God, they neither glorified him as God nor gave thanks to him, but their thinking became futile and their foolish hearts were darkened. Although they claimed to be wise, they became fools.'"

Ms. Lution looked amazed. "You mean to say that the Bible talks directly about creation science?"

"Well, yes," Billy had to smile. "The Bible tells us that God made *what we may know about him*—his eternal power and divine nature—*plain* and *clearly seen*. Through what? Through *what has been made—creation*."

"Well, can't evolution be just one theory of how God made things?"

Billy shook his head and said, "Nope!" Then he explained, "In the Bible, God makes it clear how he created. Evolution is the theory of how things *evolved*, not how they were *created*. Evolution is supposed to explain how everything came to exist naturally—*without a creator—without God*."

"Okay! Okay!" Ms. Lution said, then stood up and started pacing across the small area of the rocky ledge. "So, I guess I can see what you're saying. But why would people want to reject God?"

Billy looked Ms. Lution in the eye and answered, "I think the more important question is—why would *you* want to reject God?" Then, he stood up and left Ms. Lution to think it through by herself.

****

It didn't take Billy long to find Davy Crockett and his fellow woodsmen. They were all circling around a big tree with their binoculars to their eyes.

"So," Billy asked quietly, "is your bank robber up in that tree?"

"No." David whispered. "Look! It's one of those really big woodpeckers—a Pileated. Just listen. Each time he hits the tree, it sounds like a hammer! Incredible!"

"Man-o-man!" Darin groaned. "I get a headache just watching him. How can he keep doing that over and over?"

"Well, Darin," Billy explained, "God designed the woodpecker with a special shock absorbing piece of cartilage behind its beak. That way his brains don't turn to mush when he's pounding away at a tree. The woodpecker has all kinds of special features that enable it to do what's impossible for other birds."

David started to say something, but Abel jumped forward. "Look! Fresh tracks. Let's follow 'em!" So, off the gang went in search of the wonders of wildlife.

****

Alone on the hidden ledge, Evangeline Lution watched the wildlife down by the stream. After the grizzly family left, the small group of elk returned. Then, a family of coyotes chased a deer along the stream, only to lose it when it jumped clean over a thick mat of bushes. The young coyotes then romped and played while their parents lay down to rest.

The elk, the deer, the coyotes—each had been perfect. Each was a living being—millions of tiny parts working together to make it live, breath, run, and play. "This is ridiculous!" Evangeline said out loud. "For the random chance of evolution to produce *one* such creature is impossible, and this park is *filled* with thousands of diverse forms of wildlife!"

Then Ms. Lution realized that by looking at *what has been made*, she had come to understand what David had said—"Surely, God is the Master Designer!"

CHAPTER 15

"Wow!" David said enthusiastically. "I've never seen a live porcupine before, not even at the zoo!"

"Well," Billy said, "I think it's about time we go and get Ms. Lution, and then head back to the lodge. Carmen will be waiting for us, and we don't want to get caught out here in the dark."

However, when the group reached the hidden ledge, Ms. Lution was gone. Billy tried not to look as concerned as he felt. He calmly told Darin and David to wait on the ledge in case she would find her way back. Then, he took Abel with him to try to track her down.

Earlier, Evangeline had gone in search of the others. After having walked for about 20 minutes in one direction without finding them, she had decided to redirect her course. After another 20 minutes without finding them, she thought she'd better head back to the ledge. Suddenly, no direction seemed familiar.

Realizing she might be lost, Evangeline cupped her hands and called for help, "David! Billy James! Are you close by?"

As soon as she called, she heard something moving not too far off. Relieved, she cupped her hands to shout again. But her voice froze in her throat as she realized that the shape moving toward her was not that of a person. It was large and shaggy. It could only be a bear. Evangeline turned and ran as fast as she could.

She had hardly run a minute when the ground gave way under her and she slid down the rough slope of a slender tunnel and bumped to a hard stop about 12 feet down.

When the rocks and dirt began to settle, Evangeline realized she must have fallen into some sort of old man-made tunnel. Turning to look up from where she had fallen, she heard the snuffling approach of the curious bear. Trying not to scream, Evangeline quietly backed her way farther into the tunnel. All she could do was wait for the bear to leave.

Billy and Abel had been able to follow Ms. Lution's tracks for a time, but then lost her trail. Cupping his hands, Billy called, "Ms. Lution! Evangeline! Can you hear me?"

Without knowing it, Billy and Abel were only a couple hundred feet from Ms. Lution's underground tunnel. Unfortunately, she couldn't hear them since she was so far underground. The bear, however, did hear them and decided not to stick around and meet whatever was making all that noise. After one or two last sniffs at the strange tunnel, he lumbered away into the woods.

Billy turned to Abel. "Well, I guess we'll have to go back to the boys. I don't want to leave them too long. If she hasn't made it back there, we'll call for the rangers."

****

For the tenth time, Evangeline tried to climb up and out of the tunnel, but it was just too steep. Then she tried to dig finger and toe holes that she could use to climb out. But, after only a few holes, her fingers were raw and bleeding. Besides, she realized she couldn't venture out into the bear-inhabited woods alone in the dark. She just sat down on the ground and began to sob quietly to herself.

After a good cry, Evangeline began to think, and even to pray. "God?" she said to the darkness around her. "Did I reject you?" Almost immediately an image came to her mind. She was 15. A longtime friend had just invited her to a church revival service. A sudden, strong longing to go to the meeting rushed into her heart. But she tramped the longing down by smugly telling her friend, "No, thanks! I don't need to be born again. I was born fine the first time!"

"Why?" Evangeline asked out loud. "Why did I reject you?" Again, images filled her mind: First, her mother's casket being lowered into the ground, and her father's bitter tears; then, winning first place in the sixth-grade science contest; next, her father's praise upon her receiving the college-level Stefferd Science Award; and finally, the book she used to keep on her nightstand—*The Evolutionary Superiority of Women.*

Now, all alone in the dark, Evangeline began to understand. She had made the same fatal mistake that Eve had made in the Garden. She had listened to that bittersweet lie: "I can be equal to God. I don't need God. I don't want God." So, she had rejected God and spent her life trying to prove that she was better off without Him.

"God," Evangeline prayed, "I guess I *have* been a fool. I exchanged the truth of God for a lie. Well, now I want to reject the lie and accept your Truth."

Peace and hope filled her heart as she continued. "I believe you are my Creator and my Savior. I'm sorry for my stubborn pride. My dear mom taught me that Jesus died for my sins. Now I believe it in my heart. Teach me how to live as a Christian. Amen."

Millions upon millions of heavenly hosts gave a resounding shout of celebration as Evangeline Joy Lution left the realm of doubt and death, and soared through the gates of Eternal Life.

Evangeline also had her own small celebration, singing her mother's favorite song—Amazing Grace.

After a time, Evangeline thought she heard something through the hole above her. Standing up, she listened closely. It sounded like an animal running in her direction. No, more than one animal. Then she heard whining and growling close by. "Wolves…" she whispered, crouching back onto the floor of her little prison. Her heart began to race.

Two dog-like heads appeared and disappeared above her. Then she heard a man's voice speaking. "You two find her? Good dogs!"

Suddenly, a bright beam of light shone down the tunnel, and the man's voice asked, "You Ms. Lution, m'am? You doin' all right? My name's Cliff—Cliff Newman. I'm one of the volunteer rescue rangers here at the park." He continued, "Mr. James is just a minute behind me. We'll have you out of there quick as a wink."

****

Late the next morning, Ms. Lution joined Billy, Carmen, and Cliff by the lodge fireplace. "Good morning!" she said with a bright smile. "Where are the boys? I thought they'd be down ahead of me."

Billy winked at Cliff, then said, "Oh, I think they'll be here any second."

"Surprise!" three voices sang out together as David, Abel, and Darin popped out of their hiding places. Then, David and Abel carried something toward Ms. Lution.

"Goodness!" Ms. Lution laughed. "What is this?"

Darin answered, "It's our spay-shee-al-i-tee—our infamous four-layer-four-flavor-four-pound-cake."

"And," David piped in, "this isn't just any four-layer-four-flavor-four-pound-cake. This is your *birthday cake!*"

"How wonderful!" Ms. Lution said with tears of understanding in her eyes. "This is my first day as a brand new Christian."

Sitting by the lodge's big picture window, they all enjoyed a piece (or two) of the super-fan-delicious cake while laughing and talking.

After a while, Darin turned to Cliff. "I way liked those dogs you used last night to track down Miss Eva—big, strong, smart, brave. But, I couldn't figure out what they were."

"The park keeps several search and rescue dogs. Brindy, Spud, and Blacky are all Labradoodles—part Labrador Retriever and part Standard Poodle. Blacky's a full 100 pounds. It's good to have dogs with a bit of weight on them since there are wolves around."

Abel stood up and sauntered over to Darin. "See thar Mr. Smarty-pants. Thar do be designer dogs that a man of the wild woods can be proud to own."

Darin rolled his eyes and grumbled. "I don't think Davy Crockett would call anyone *Mr. Smarty-pants*."

Mrs. James started to gather empty cake plates. "So, David, what animal *are* you going to pick for your science report?"

Darin leaped off his chair and began to soar around the room. "The bald eagle," he said. "Majesty in mo…"

"David," Billy broke in. "Think of the power, the raw beauty of the grizzly…"

Something at the window caught David's eye as Billy and Darin continued their good-natured argument. A large bird—with its telltale red cap—flew to a branch right in front of David. The bird looked him right in the eye and winked. David smiled and winked back. Then the woodpecker flew off.

"Give it up, you guys," David said, turning to his friends. "I've already decided on something really special."

CHAPTER 16

The Complexity of Life
(What a Grand Design!)

by David J. Avila

Introduction

The complexity of life refers to different parts within a single living organism working together in an amazing and wonderful way. For example, a bird has a heart that pumps blood to the lungs and the brain, lungs that give oxygen to the brain and the heart, and a brain that controls the heart and lungs. All three parts must be in place for the bird to live. If one part is missing, the bird can't exist.

Scientists have come up with two different theories about how this complexity of life came about. Both theories start with the same observable facts, but end with very different conclusions. The reason they come to such different conclusions is that each theory is based on a vastly different premise (beginning belief).

Evolution is based on the belief that random natural processes (mutations and natural selection) over millions of years have produced the amazing complexity of life we observe today. *Creation* is based on the belief that a Creator (the God of the Bible) originally designed His creation with the complexity of life we observe today.

For this report, I will look at some characteristics of birds in general, and then focus on one bird in particular. I will show that my animal, the woodpecker, does *not* fit into evolution's theory of random natural processes. I will show that the woodpecker's amazing characteristics are best explained by God's creative design as described in the Bible.

Birds from Reptiles?

Evolution claims that a single-celled organism changed over millions of years into a flying bird. There was no plan, no purpose, no design—just random natural processes. Of course, from blob to bird would take many, many evolutionary *steps* of change. But let's just look at one of the most celebrated steps—reptile to bird.

Both reptiles and birds have hearts, lungs, and brains. Both have bones, stomachs, and skin. Both eat, sleep, and lay eggs. It would seem that not much change is needed to *evolve* from reptile to bird. Maybe just grow a few feathers, right?

But reptiles are naturally *very* different from birds. Flying birds have streamlined bodies that are balanced for flight—reptiles do not. Birds have hollow, lightweight bones that are a working part of their breathing system—reptiles do not. Birds have strong muscles and specially designed long tendons to give them power for flight—reptiles do not. Birds have all these characteristics, designed perfectly for flight, but reptiles have none of them. Birds also have two other special structures that make them *immensely* different from reptiles.

Feathers

Evolutionists claim that bird feathers evolved from reptile scales. But look at the evidence. Feathers are strong, lightweight, and aerodynamic. They have barbs and hooks, like Velcro, that make them waterproof and easily preened back to their aerodynamic shape. Feathers are perfectly designed for flight. But scales are just folds in a reptile's skin, perfectly designed for the reptile, but certainly not for flight.

According to evolution, scales evolved into feathers by random natural processes—step by step. There was no plan, no purpose, no design—just random natural processes. Each evolutionary step would have to produce a useful, functioning scale/feather thing that had a greater advantage over the previous step. A *transitional form* would be an animal that possessed *things* on it that are somewhere in between a scale and a feather. If evolution were true, we would expect to find many transitional forms, but not one transitional form has ever been found, either living, or in the fossil record.

Observable, testable, repeatable science shows that evolution's random natural processes (mutations and natural selection) do *not* produce new information. The information to form feathers is not present in reptiles, but is present in birds. So, for scales to evolve into feathers, *a lot* of genetic information had to be added. But if evolution's random natural processes do not produce new information, then how could the new feather information have been added? It makes more sense to believe that feathers were perfectly *designed* (by a Creator) for flight.

Bird Lungs

Evolutionists also assume that reptile lungs evolved into bird lungs. But these two types of lungs are vastly different.

Huge changes would be needed to turn one into the other. Reptiles (similar to humans) have a bellows-like lung. These lungs expand and draw air into tiny sacs. There, blood picks up oxygen and gets rid of carbon dioxide. Then the lungs contract and the air is forced out of the lungs the same way it came in. This design works very well for reptiles.

But bird lungs don't work that way. They don't expand and contract like a bellows. Instead, birds have a system of air sacs that keeps the air flowing *in one direction* through the lung—not in and out. The blood that picks up oxygen from the lungs flows in the opposite direction of the air flowing through. This is known as *counter-current exchange.* It is a very well-designed lung that gives birds the added energy they need to fly.

Evolution claims that reptile lungs evolved into bird lungs through random natural processes—step by step. There was no plan, no purpose, no design—just random natural processes. Each step would have to produce a working lung that would have an advantage over the previous step. A *transitional form* would be an animal with lungs that are somewhere in between reptile lungs and bird lungs. If evolution were true, we should find many transitional forms, but no transitional form has ever been observed, either living, or in the fossil record. In fact, no scientist (that I've ever heard of) can even imagine how such a transitional lung would function.

Evolutionists can *believe* that the reptile lung evolved into the bird lung. But it's just a belief! There is no observable science to support this belief. It makes more sense to believe that bird lungs were perfectly *designed* (by a Creator) for birds.

The Woodpecker

Now, let's go from the characteristics of birds in general to one specific kind of bird—the woodpecker. A close look at the woodpecker will show that it was wonderfully designed by God the Creator.

To find food, some woodpeckers hammer a tree at the rate of 15 times *per second.* The force it uses is 1,000 times the force of gravity. To withstand this, its special chisel-tipped beak is stronger than most other birds. Also, its skull is thicker, for its body weight, than any other animal, and in between its beak and skull is a cartilage *shock-absorber*. All of this makes the woodpecker's head perfectly designed for pecking out holes in trees.

Next, unlike most other birds (who have three toes in front and one in back), the woodpecker has two toes in front and two in back. It also has special, stiff tail feathers with spines on the tips that act like a third leg. Together, the woodpecker's special feet and tail feathers are perfect for climbing and for holding a steady position while pecking.

Finally, the woodpecker's tongue is extra long and has a barb at the end so it can reach in a hole and stab a bug to bring it out. Its tongue also produces a special glue at the end to keep the bug attached. Then, when the tongue brings the bug back in the beak, a special chemical dissolves the glue so the bug can be eaten.

But, there's still more! The tongue of most birds is anchored in the back of its beak, but a woodpecker's beak is too long. Its tongue is anchored in the nostril. The tongue starts there, then passes up, over, and around the back of the skull, then comes around and up into the beak. This extra long tongue is perfectly designed for reaching into a hole in a tree, and then is rolled up and stored in the nostril.

Evolutionists can *believe* that random natural processes—with no plan, no purpose, and no design—changed a single-celled organism into a perfectly designed woodpecker. But evidence, observation, and logic lead *me* to believe that the woodpecker was wonderfully created by God.

Conclusion

The two main theories explaining the complexity of life begin with *very* different beliefs. Evolution believes that random natural processes over millions of years have produced the amazing complexity of life we observe today. Creationists believe that God's original design explains the amazing complexity of life we observe today. So, which theory explains the evidence (the woodpecker) better?

The woodpecker's streamlined body, lightweight hollow bones, strong muscles, and special long tendons are all perfectly designed for flight. Its feathers are lightweight, strong, and keep their aerodynamic shape easily because of special barbs and hooks, all perfectly designed for flight. The woodpecker's special counter-current lungs are unique and perfectly designed for the energy needed to fly. And its special beak and skull, special toes and tail, and super-special tongue are all perfectly designed for catching and eating bugs out of the holes it pecks in trees.

Random (brainless) natural processes cannot even begin to explain the perfect design of the woodpecker. The evidence is best explained by God's creative design as described in the Bible. The woodpecker—what a grand design!

****

Evangeline was disappointed, but not surprised, as she read her father's response to her last several e-mails:

TO: evalution@science.qlu.net
FROM: drevlution@science.qlu.net
RE: extended leave of absence

Eva,

What on earth has come over you? You cannot really mean that you are giving up all you have learned and earned—all that has made me so proud of you—to believe this creation nonsense.

No. The stress of your demanding job must be affecting your decisions. I insist that you take an extended leave of absence. Rest. Have time to restore your good sense.

I'm sorry to inform you that the School Board has decided that, in your current state of mind, you will not be able to continue as principal at Darwin Middle School. We must consider your influence on the students. I, myself, therefore, will be filling your position until you can assure us that you do indeed stand firmly on the scientifically solid ground of evolution.

Your leave of absence is effective immediately.

Your father,
Dr. E. V. Lution

Evangeline smiled sadly to herself. She knew that the School Board's decision was not legal. They couldn't force her out of her position based on her religious beliefs.

However, she was ready for a break. A sabbatical sounded good. She needed time to build up a strong foundation in her newfound faith. She had a lot of questions and now she knew where to start looking for the answers—first of all, in the Bible. But there were also a growing number of creation resources that could help her on her journey.

In the meantime, Eva would pray for her father to open his heart to exchange the lie of evolution for the Truth of God.

A NOTE FROM DAVID

Hola Compañeros!

This is David Avila. I just wanted to share two important things *I've* learned so far this school year.

First, it's important to remember that *our battle is not against flesh and blood.* That means, if someone disagrees with you or challenges what you believe, don't get upset or angry. An argument will only make things worse. I've learned that speaking with respect is the key to mutual understanding and a good relationship for future discussions.

Second, don't be afraid to *ask for help* in looking for answers. I was just about ready to give up until Billy and the T-twins came along. And, it turns out that my parents were an excellent resource, too. My dad directed me to several good creation science websites, such as CREATION.com. These sites had links to great articles, books, videos, even music about the *creation/evolution debate.* Don't be afraid—ask questions and do further research!

Gracia!
David

ABOUT THE AUTHORS

John is a nationally certified middle school teacher. He has worked with teenagers for the past 20 years, both as a teacher and as a youth pastor. Lisa received her college degree in English Literature. She has also been active working with youth for the past 20 years. The Foxes live on a ten-acre farm in Central Ohio where they homeschool their six children. They also own lots of dogs and a variety of fun farm animals.

Authors' Note

Although this book is a work of fiction, the scientific evidence discussed is *real* and is available to everyone. Evolution's bold 'scientific' claims have clear religious implications against faith in God and His Word. Our goal is simply to provide real scientific evidence that refutes evolution's claims and upholds the Word of God from beginning to end. We encourage our readers to ask questions and to do further research.

Always remember that we are *not* looking for evidence to *prove* the Bible. We believe that the Bible is true. Therefore, we believe that God's Word is the best foundation for understanding *all* the science we discover in the world and in the universe.

RECOMMENDED RESOURCES:

THE CREATION ANSWERS BOOK

The Creation Answers Book provides biblical answers to over 60 important questions that everyone wants to know about creation/evolution and the Bible like "What about dinosaurs, carbon 14 dating, and who was Cain's wife?". Not only will it answer your questions, but it will equip you to effectively respond to the questions of others. This important work is a 'must have' for anyone's library.

EXPLORING GEOLOGY WITH MR. HIBB

This wonderfully illustrated, full-color book provides a biblical view of geology for elementary/primary school ages. It follows the entertaining adventures of the curious grasshopper, Mr Hibb, as he makes the learning of geology delightful and faith building.

REFUTING EVOLUTION

Refuting Evolution is a hard-hitting critique of the most up-to-date arguments for evolution, to challenge educators, students, and parents. It is a powerful yet concise summary of the arguments against evolution and for creation. It will stimulate much discussion and help students and teachers think more critically about origins.

TYLER CRAY AND THE GRAND CANYON BIRTHDAY

Young Tyler Cray has been looking forward to going on vacation to the Canyon for such a long time! When he finally arrives, the sight of it is far more splendid than he imagined. He learns much about this incredible, scenic place (including some terrific faith-building, scientific information).

COMIC BOOKS

'Everybody reads comics'—so, what a great way to reach youth and old alike. Beautifully illustrated and full of information, these are great booklets to give to those who may shun the conventional creationist material. Each closes with a powerful salvation message.

GOO 2 U, VIA THE ZOO DVD

Dave and Dan set out to open up the big questions to a searching generation of youth. Challenging, fun, and culturally relevant, this DVD offers a way out of the confusion for youth who are searching for answers that satisfy both the mind and the heart.

CREATION.com

For more information on creation/evolution and Bible-science issues

---

AUSTRALIA
Creation Ministries International (Australia)
PO Box 4545
Eight Mile Plains, QLD 4113

Phone: (07) 3340 9888
Fax: (07) 3340 9889
ABN 31 010 120 304

CANADA
Creation Ministries International (Canada)
300 Mill St, Unit 7
Kitchener, ON N2M 5G8

Phone: (519) 746–7616
Orders & donations: 1-888-251-5360
Fax: (519) 746–7617

NEW ZEALAND
Creation Ministries International (NZ)
PO Box 39005
Howick, Auckland 2145

Phone/Fax: (09) 537 4818
A Registered Charitable Trust

SINGAPORE
Creation Ministries International (Singapore)
Clementi Central Post Office
PO Box 195
Singapore 911207

Phone: 9698 4292

SOUTH AFRICA
Creation Ministries International (SA)
PO Box 3349
Durbanville 7551

Phone: (021) 979 0107
Fax: (086) 519 0555

UK & Europe
Creation Ministries International (UK/Europe)
15 Station St,
Whetstone, Leicestershire, LE8 6JS

Phone: 0116-2848-999

USA
Creation Ministries International (USA)
PO Box 350,
Powder Springs, GA 30127

Phone: (800) 616-1264
Fax: (770) 439-9784

OTHER COUNTRIES
Creation Ministries International
PO Box 4545
Eight Mile Plains,
QLD 4113, Australia

Phone: +617 3340 9888
Fax: +617 3340 9889